'Ah, what is the life of a human being – a drop of dew, a flash of lightning? This is so sad, so sad.'

RYŪNOSUKE AKUTAGAWA

The Life of a Stupid Man

Translated by
Jay Rubin

Contents

In a Bamboo Grove

THE TESTIMONY OF A WOODCUTTER UNDER QUESTIONING BY THE MAGISTRATE

That is true, Your Honor. I am the one who found the body. I went out as usual this morning to cut cedar in the hills behind my place. The body was in a bamboo grove on the other side of the mountain. Its exact location? A few hundred yards off the Yamashina post road. A deserted place where a few scrub cedar trees are mixed in with the bamboo.

The man was lying on his back in his pale blue robe with the sleeves tied up and one of those fancy Kyoto-style black hats with the sharp creases. He had only one stab wound, but it was right in the middle of his chest; the bamboo leaves around the body were soaked with dark red blood. No, the bleeding had stopped. The wound looked dry, and I remember it had a big horsefly sucking on it so hard the thing didn't even notice my footsteps.

Did I see a sword or anything? No, Sir, not a thing. Just a length of rope by the cedar tree next to the body.

And – oh yes, there was a comb there, too. Just the rope and the comb is all. But the weeds and the bamboo leaves on the ground were pretty trampled down: he must have put up a tremendous fight before they killed him. How's that, Sir – a horse? No, a horse could never have gotten into that place. It's all bamboo thicket between there and the road.

THE TESTIMONY OF A TRAVELING PRIEST UNDER QUESTIONING BY THE MAGISTRATE

I'm sure I passed the man yesterday, Your Honor. Yesterday at – about noon, I'd say. Near Checkpoint Hill on the way to Yamashina. He was walking toward the checkpoint with a woman on horseback. She wore a stiff, round straw hat with a long veil hanging down around the brim; I couldn't see her face, just her robe. I think it had a kind of dark-red outer layer with a blue-green lining. The horse was a dappled gray with a tinge of red, and I'm fairly sure it had a clipped mane. Was it a big horse? I'd say it was a few inches taller than most, but I'm a priest after all. I don't know much about horses. The man? No, Sir, he had a good-sized sword, and he was equipped with a bow and arrows. I can still see that black-lacquered quiver of his: he must have had twenty arrows in it, maybe more. I would never have dreamt that a thing like this could happen to such a man. Ah, what is the life of a human being – a drop of dew, a flash of lightning? This is so sad, so sad. What can I say?

THE TESTIMONY OF A POLICEMAN UNDER QUESTIONING BY THE MAGISTRATE

The man I captured, Your Honor? I am certain he is the famous bandit, Tajōmaru. True, when I caught him he had fallen off his horse, and he was moaning and groaning on the stone bridge at Awataguchi. The time, Sir? It was last night at the first watch. He was wearing the same dark blue robe and carrying the same long sword he used the time I almost captured him before. You can see he also has a bow and arrows now. Oh, is that so, Sir? The dead man, too? That settles it, then: I'm sure this Tajōmaru fellow is the murderer. A leather-wrapped bow, a quiver in black lacquer, seventeen hawk-feather arrows – they must have belonged to the victim. And yes, as you say, Sir, the horse is a dappled gray with a touch of red, and it has a clipped mane. It's only a dumb animal, but it gave that bandit just what he deserved, throwing him like that. It was a short way beyond the bridge, trailing its reins on the ground and eating plume grass by the road.

Of all the bandits prowling around Kyoto, this Tajōmaru is known as a fellow who likes the women. Last fall, people at Toribe Temple found a pair of worshippers murdered – a woman and a child – on the hill behind the statue of Binzuru. Everybody said Tajōmaru must have done it. If it turns out he killed the man, there's no telling what he might have done to the woman who was on the horse. I don't mean to meddle, Sir, but I do think you ought to question him about that.

THE TESTIMONY OF AN OLD WOMAN UNDER QUESTIONING BY THE MAGISTRATE

Yes, Your Honor, my daughter was married to the dead man. He is not from the capital, though. He was a samurai serving in the Wakasa provincial office. His name was Kanazawa no Takehiro, and he was twenty-six years old. No, Sir, he was a very kind man. I can't believe anyone would have hated him enough to do this.

My daughter, Sir? Her name is Masago, and she is nineteen years old. She's as bold as any man, but the only man she has ever known is Takehiro. Her complexion is a little on the dark side, and she has a mole by the outside corner of her left eye, but her face is a tiny, perfect oval.

Takehiro left for Wakasa yesterday with my daughter, but what turn of fate could have led to this? There's nothing I can do for my son-in-law anymore, but what could have happened to my daughter? I'm worried sick about her. Oh please, Sir, do everything you can to find her, leave no stone unturned: I have lived a long time, but I have never wanted anything so badly in my life. Oh how I hate that bandit – that, that Tajōmaru! Not only my son-in-law, but my daughter . . . (Here the old woman broke down and was unable to go on speaking.)

* * * * *

TAJŌMARU'S CONFESSION

Sure, I killed the man. But I didn't kill the woman. So, where did she go? I don't know any better than you do. Now, wait just a minute – you can torture me all you want, but I can't tell you what I don't know. And besides, now that you've got me, I'm not going to hide anything. I'm no coward.

I met that couple yesterday, a little after noon. The second I saw them, a puff of wind lifted her veil and I caught a peek at her. Just a peek: that's maybe why she looked so perfect to me – an absolute bodhisattva of a woman. I made up my mind right then to take her even if I had to kill the man.

Oh come on, killing a man is not as big a thing as people like you seem to think. If you're going to take somebody's woman, a man has to die. When *I* kill a man, I do it with my sword, but people like you don't use swords. You gentlemen kill with your power, with your money, and sometimes just with your words: you tell people you're doing them a favor. True, no blood flows, the man is still alive, but you've killed him all the same. I don't know whose sin is greater – yours or mine. (A sarcastic smile.)

Of course, if you can take the woman without killing the man, all the better. Which is exactly what I was hoping to do yesterday. It would have been impossible on the Yamashina post road, of course, so I thought of a way to lure them into the hills.

It was easy. I fell in with them on the road and made up a story. I told them I had found an old burial mound in the hills, and when I opened it it was full of swords and mirrors and things. I said I had buried the stuff in a bamboo grove on the other side of the mountain to keep anyone from finding out about it, and I'd sell it cheap to the right buyer. He started getting interested soon enough. It's scary what greed can do to people, don't you think? In less than an hour, I was leading that couple and their horse up a mountain trail.

When we reached the grove, I told them the treasure was buried in there and they should come inside with me and look at it. The man was so hungry for the stuff by then, he couldn't refuse, but the woman said she'd wait there on the horse. I figured that would happen – the woods are so thick. They fell right into my trap. We left the woman alone and went into the grove.

It was all bamboo at first. Fifty yards or so inside, there was a sort of open clump of cedars – the perfect place for what I was going to do. I pushed through the thicket and made up some nonsense about how the treasure was buried under one of them. When he heard that, the man charged toward some scrawny cedars visible up ahead. The bamboo thinned out, and the trees were standing there in a row. As soon as we got to them, I grabbed him and pinned him down. I could see he was a strong man – he carried a sword – but I took him by surprise, and he couldn't do a thing. I had him tied to the base of a tree in no time. Where did I get the rope? Well, I'm a thief, you know – I might have to scale a wall at any time – so I've always got a piece of rope in my belt. I stuffed his mouth full of bamboo leaves to keep him quiet. That's all there was to it.

Once I finished with the man, I went and told the woman that her husband had suddenly been taken ill and she should come and have a look at him. This was another bull's-eye, of course. She took off her hat and let me lead her by the hand into the grove. As soon as she saw the man tied to the tree, though, she whipped a dagger out of her breast. I never saw a woman with such fire! If I'd been off my guard, she'd have stuck that thing in my gut. And the way she kept coming, she would have done me some damage eventually no matter how much I dodged. Still, I *am* Tajōmaru. One way or another, I managed to knock the knife out of her hand without drawing my sword. Even the most spirited woman is going to be helpless if she hasn't got a weapon. And so I was able to make the woman mine without taking her husband's life.

Yes, you heard me: without taking her husband's life. I wasn't planning to kill him on top of everything else. The woman was on the ground, crying, and I was getting ready to run out of the grove and leave her there when all of a sudden she grabbed my arm like some kind of crazy person. And then I heard what she was shouting between sobs. She could hardly catch her breath: 'Either you die or my husband dies. It has to be one of you. It's worse than death for me to have two men see my shame. I want to stay with the one left alive, whether it's you or him.' That gave me a wild desire to kill her husband. (Sullen excitement.)

When I say this, you probably think I'm crueler than you are. But that's because you didn't see the look on her face – and especially, you never saw the way her eyes were burning at that moment. When those eyes met mine, I knew I wanted to make her my wife. Let the thunder god kill me, I'd make her my wife – that was the only thought in my head. And no, not just from lust. I know that's what you gentlemen are thinking. If lust was all I felt for her, I'd already taken care of that. I could've just kicked her down and gotten out of there. And the man wouldn't have stained my sword with his blood. But the moment my eyes locked onto hers in that dark grove, I knew I couldn't leave there until I had killed him.

Still, I didn't want to kill him in a cowardly way. I untied him and challenged him to a sword fight. (That piece of rope they found was the one I threw aside then.) The man looked furious as he drew his big sword, and without a word he sprang at me in a rage. I don't have to tell you the outcome of the fight. My sword pierced his breast on the twenty-third thrust. Not till the twenty-third: I want you to keep that in mind. I still admire him for that. He's the only man who ever lasted even twenty thrusts with me. (Cheerful grin.)

As he went down, I lowered my bloody sword and turned toward the woman. But she was gone! I looked for her among the cedars, but the bamboo leaves on the ground showed no sign she'd ever been there. I cocked my ear for any sound of her, but all I could hear was the man's death rattle.

Maybe she had run through the underbrush to call for help when the sword fight started. The thought made me fear for my life. I grabbed the man's sword and his bow and arrows and headed straight for the mountain road. The woman's horse was still there, just chewing on grass. Anything else I could tell you after that would be a waste of breath. I got rid of his sword before coming to Kyoto, though.

So that's my confession. I always knew my head would end up hanging in the tree outside the prison some day, so let me have the ultimate punishment. (Defiant attitude.)

PENITENT CONFESSION OF A WOMAN IN THE KIYOMIZU TEMPLE

After the man in the dark blue robe had his way with me, he looked at my husband, all tied up, and taunted him with laughter. How humiliated my husband must have felt! He squirmed and twisted in the ropes that covered his body, but the knots ate all the deeper into his flesh. Stumbling, I ran to his side. No – I *tried* to run to him, but instantly the man kicked me down. And that was when it happened: that was when I saw the indescribable glint in my husband's eyes. Truly, it was indescribable. It makes me shudder to recall it even now. My husband was unable to speak a word, and yet, in that moment, his eyes conveyed his whole heart to me. What I saw shining there was neither anger nor sorrow. It was the cold flash of contempt – contempt for *me*. This struck me more painfully than the bandit's kick. I let out a cry and collapsed on the spot.

When I regained consciousness, the man in blue was gone. The only one there in the grove was my husband, still tied to the cedar tree. I just barely managed to raise myself on the carpet of dead bamboo leaves, and look into my husband's face. His eyes were exactly as they had been before, with that same cold look of contempt and hatred. How can I describe the emotion that filled my heart then? Shame . . . sorrow . . . anger . . . I staggered over to him.

'Oh, my husband! Now that this has happened, I

cannot go on living with you. I am prepared to die here and now. But you – yes, I want you to die as well. You witnessed my shame. I cannot leave you behind with that knowledge.'

I struggled to say everything I needed to say, but my husband simply went on staring at me in disgust. I felt as if my breast would burst open at any moment, but holding my feelings in check, I began to search the bamboo thicket for his sword. The bandit must have taken it – I couldn't find it anywhere – and my husband's bow and arrows were gone as well. But then I had the good luck to find the dagger at my feet. I brandished it before my husband and spoke to him once again.

'This is the end, then. Please be so good as to allow me to take your life. I will quickly follow you in death.'

When he heard this, my husband finally began moving his lips. Of course his mouth was stuffed with bamboo leaves, so he couldn't make a sound, but I knew immediately what he was saying. With total contempt for me, he said only, 'Do it.' Drifting somewhere between dream and reality, I thrust the dagger through the chest of his pale blue robe.

Then I lost consciousness again. When I was able to look around me at last, my husband, still tied to the tree, was no longer breathing. Across his ashen face shone a streak of light from the setting sun, filtered through the bamboo and cedar. Gulping back my tears, I untied him and cast the rope aside. And then – and then what happened to me? I no longer have the strength to tell it. That I failed to kill myself is obvious. I tried to stab myself in the throat. I threw myself in a pond at the foot of the mountain. Nothing worked. I am still here, by no means proud of my inability to die. (Forlorn smile.) Perhaps even Kanzeon, bodhisattva of compassion, has turned away from me for being so weak. But now – now that I have killed my husband, now that I have been violated by a bandit – what am I to do? Tell me, what am I to . . . (Sudden violent sobbing.)

THE TESTIMONY OF THE DEAD MAN'S SPIRIT TOLD THROUGH A MEDIUM

After the bandit had his way with my wife, he sat there on the ground, trying to comfort her. I could say nothing, of course, and I was bound to the cedar tree. But I kept trying to signal her with my eyes: *Don't believe anything he tells you. He's lying, no matter what he says*. I tried to convey my meaning to her, but she just went on cringing there on the fallen bamboo leaves, staring at her knees. And, you know, I could see she was listening to him. I writhed with jealousy, but the bandit kept his smooth talk going from one point to the next. 'Now that your flesh has been sullied, things will never be the same with your husband. Don't stay with him – come and be my wife! It's because

I love you so much that I was so wild with you.' The bandit had the gall to speak to her like that!

When my wife raised her face in response to him, she seemed almost spellbound. I had never seen her look so beautiful as she did at that moment. And what do you think this beautiful wife of mine said to the bandit, in my presence – in the presence of her husband bound hand and foot? My spirit may be wandering now between one life and the next, but every time I recall her answer, I burn with indignation. 'All right,' she told him, 'take me anywhere you like.' (Long silence.)

And that was not her only crime against me. If that were all she did, I would not be suffering so here in the darkness. With him leading her by the hand, she was stepping out of the bamboo grove as if in a dream, when suddenly the color drained from her face and she pointed back to me. 'Kill him!' she screamed. 'Kill him! I can't be with you as long as he is alive!' Again and again she screamed, as if she had lost her mind, 'Kill him!' Even now her words like a windstorm threaten to blow me headlong into the darkest depths. Have such hateful words ever come from the mouth of a human being before? Have such damnable words ever reached the ears of a human being before? Have such – (An explosion of derisive laughter.) Even the bandit went pale when he heard her. She clung to his arm and screamed again, 'Kill him!' The bandit stared at her, saying neither that he would kill me nor that he would not. The next thing I knew, however, he sent my wife sprawling on the bamboo leaves with a single kick. (Another explosion of derisive laughter.) The bandit calmly folded his arms and turned to look at me.

'What do you want me to do with her?' he asked. 'Kill her or let her go? Just nod to answer. Kill her?' For this if for nothing else, I am ready to forgive the bandit his crimes. (Second long silence.)

When I hesitated with my answer, my wife let out a scream and darted into the depths of the bamboo thicket. He sprang after her, but I don't think he even managed to lay a hand on her sleeve. I watched the spectacle as if it were some kind of vision.

After my wife ran off, the bandit picked up my sword and bow and arrows, and he cut my ropes at one place. 'Now it's my turn to run,' I remember hearing him mutter as he disappeared from the thicket. Then the whole area was quiet. No – I could hear someone weeping. While I was untying myself, I listened to the sound, until I realized – I realized that I was the one crying. (Another long silence.)

I finally raised myself, exhausted, from the foot of the tree. Lying there before me was the dagger that my wife had dropped. I picked it up and shoved it into my chest. Some kind of bloody mass rose to my mouth, but I felt no pain at all. My chest grew cold, and then everything sank into stillness. What perfect silence! In the skies above that grove on the hidden side of the mountain, not a single bird came to sing. The lonely glow of the sun lingered among the high branches of cedar and bamboo. The sun – but gradually, even that began to fade, and with it the cedars and bamboo. I lay there wrapped in a deep silence.

Then stealthy footsteps came up to me. I tried to see who it was, but the darkness had closed in all around me. Someone – that someone gently pulled the dagger from my chest with an invisible hand. Again a rush of blood filled my mouth, but then I sank once and for all into the darkness between lives.

Death Register

1

My mother was a madwoman. I never did feel close to her, as a son should feel toward his mother. Hair held in place by a comb, she would sit alone all day puffing on a long, skinny pipe in the house of my birth family in Tokyo's Shiba Ward. She had a tiny face on a tiny body, and that face of hers, for some reason, was always ashen and lifeless. Once, reading *The Story of the Western Wing*, I came upon the phrase 'smell of earth, taste of mud', and thought immediately of my mother – of her emaciated face in profile.

And so I never had the experience of a mother's care. I do seem to recall that one time, when my adoptive mother made a point of taking me upstairs to see her, she suddenly conked me on the head with her pipe. In general, though, she was a quiet lunatic. I or my elder sister would sometimes press her to paint a picture for us, and she would do it on a sheet of paper folded in four. And not just with black ink, either. She would apply my sister's watercolors to blossoming plants or the costumes of children on an outing. The people in her pictures, though, always had fox faces.

My mother died in the autumn of my eleventh year, not so much from illness, I think, as from simply wasting away. I have a fairly clear memory of the events surrounding her death.

A telegram must have arrived to alert us. Late on a windless night, I climbed into a rickshaw with my adoptive mother and sped across the city from Honjo to Shiba. Otherwise in my life I have never used a scarf, but I do recall that on that particular night I had a thin silk handkerchief wrapped around my neck. I also recall that it had some kind of Chinese landscape motif, and that it smelled strongly of Iris Bouquet.

My mother lay on a futon in the eight-mat parlor directly beneath her upstairs room. I knelt beside her, wailing, with my four-year-older sister. I felt especially miserable when I heard someone behind me say, 'The end is near.' My mother had been lying there as good as dead, but suddenly she opened her eyes and spoke. Sad as everyone felt, we couldn't help giggling.

I stayed up by my mother through the following night as well, but that night, for some reason, my tears simply wouldn't flow. Ashamed to be so unfeeling while right next to me my sister wept almost constantly, I struggled to pretend. Yet I also believed that as long as I was unable to cry, my mother would not die.

On the evening of the third day, though, she did die, with very little suffering. A few times before it happened, she would seem to regain consciousness, look us all in the face, and release an endless stream of tears, but as usual she said not a thing.

Even after her body had been placed in the coffin, I couldn't keep from breaking down time and again. The old woman we called our 'Ōji Auntie', a distant relative, would say, 'I'm so impressed with you!' My only thought was that here was a person who let herself be impressed by very strange things.

The day of my mother's funeral, my sister climbed into a rickshaw holding the memorial tablet, and I followed her inside, holding the censer. I dozed off now and then, waking with a start each time the censer was about to drop from my hand. Still, we seemed never to reach Yanaka. Always I would wake to find the long funeral procession still winding its way through the streets of Tokyo in the autumn sunlight.

The anniversary of my mother's death is 28 November. The priest gave her the posthumous name of Kimyōin Myōjō Nisshin Daishi. I can remember neither the anniversary of my birth father's death two decades later nor his posthumous name. Memorizing such things had probably been a matter of pride for me at the age of eleven.

2

I have just the one elder sister. Not very healthy, she is nevertheless the mother of two children. She is not, of course, one of those I want to include in this 'Death Register.' Rather, it is the sister who died suddenly just before I was born. Among us three siblings, she was said to be the smartest.

She was certainly the first – which is why they named her 'Hatsuko' (First Daughter). Even now a small framed portrait of 'Little Hatsu' adorns the Buddhist altar in my house. There is nothing at all sickly-looking about her. Her cheeks, with their little dimples, are as round as ripe apricots.

Little Hatsu was by far the one who received the greatest outpouring of love from my parents. They made a point of sending her all the way from Shiba Shinsenza to attend the kindergarten of a Mrs Summers – I think it was – in Tsukiji. On weekends, though, she would stay with my mother's family, the Akutagawas, in Honjo. On these outings of hers, Little Hatsu would probably wear Western dresses, which still, in the Meiji twenties, would have seemed very modish. When I was in elementary school, I remember, I used to get remnants of her clothes to put on my rubber doll. Without exception, all the cloth patches were imported calico scattered with tiny printed flowers or musical instruments.

One Sunday afternoon in early spring, when Little Hatsu was strolling through the garden (wearing a Western dress, as I imagine her), she called out to our aunt Fuki in the parlor, 'Auntie, what's the name of this tree?'

'Which one?'

'This one, with the buds.'

In the garden of my mother's family, a single low *boke** trailed its branches over the old well. Little Hatsu, in pigtails, was probably looking up at its thorny branches with big round eyes.

'It has the same name as you,' my aunt said, but before she could explain her joke, Hatsu made up one of her own:

'Then it must be a "dummy" tree.'

My aunt always tells this story whenever the conversation turns to Little Hatsu. Indeed, it's the only story left to tell about her. Probably not too many days later, Little Hatsu was in her coffin. I don't remember the posthumous name engraved on her tiny memorial tablet. I do have a strangely clear memory of her death date, though: 5 April.

For some unknown reason, I feel close to this sister I never knew. If 'Little Hatsu' were still living, she would

* *boke*: The name of the tree, known as a Japanese quince (*Pyrus japonica*) in English, is a homonym for 'dimwit'. Before the aunt can joke with her that both she and the tree are '*boke*', Hatsu cleverly makes up her own remarkably similar word play using '*baka*' (dummy).

be over forty now. And maybe, at that age, she would look like my mother as I recall her upstairs in the Shiba house, blankly puffing away on her pipe. I often feel as if there is a fortyish woman somewhere – a phantom not exactly my mother nor this dead sister – watching over my life. Could this be the effect of nerves wracked by coffee and tobacco? Or might it be the work of some supernatural power giving occasional glimpses of itself to the real world?

3

Because my mother lost her mind, I was adopted into the family of her elder brother shortly after I was born, and so my real father was another parent for whom I had little feeling. He owned a dairy and seems to have been a small-scale success. That father was the person who taught me all about the newly imported fruits and drinks of the day: *banana*, *ice cream*, *pineapple*, *rum* – and probably much more. I remember once drinking rum in the shade of an oak tree outside the pasture, which was then located in Shinjuku. Rum was an amber-colored drink with little alcohol.

When I was very young, my father would try to entice me back from my adoptive family by plying me with these rare treats. I remember how he once openly tempted me into running away while feeding me ice cream in the Uoei restaurant in Ōmori. At times like this he could be a smooth talker and exude real charm. Unfortunately for him, though, his enticements never worked. This was because I loved my adoptive family too much – and especially my mother's elder sister, Aunt Fuki.

My father had a short temper and was always fighting with people. When I was in the third year of middle school, I beat him at sumo wrestling by tripping him backwards using a special judo move of mine. He got up and came right after me saying 'One more go.' I threw him easily again. He came charging at me for a third time, again saying 'One more go,' but now I could see he was angry. My other aunt (Aunt Fuyu, my mother's younger sister – by then my father's second wife) was watching all this, and she winked at me a few times behind my father's back. After grappling with him for a little while, I purposely fell over backwards. I'm sure if I hadn't lost to him, I would have ended up another victim of my father's temper.

When I was twenty-eight and still teaching, I received a telegram saying 'Father hospitalized,' and I rushed from Kamakura to Tokyo. He was in the Tokyo Hospital with influenza. I spent the next three days there with my Aunts Fuyu and Fuki, sleeping in a corner of the room. I was beginning to feel bored when a call came for me from an Irish reporter friend inviting me out for a meal at a Tsukiji tea house. Using his upcoming departure for America as an excuse, I left for Tsukiji even though my father was on the verge of death.

We had a delightful Japanese dinner in the company of four or five geisha. I think the meal ended around ten o'clock. Leaving the reporter, I was headed down the steep, narrow stairway when, from behind, I heard a soft feminine voice calling me 'Ah-san' in that playful geisha way. I stopped in mid-descent and turned to look up toward the top of the stairs. There, one of the geisha was looking down, her eyes fixed on mine. Wordlessly, I continued down the stairs and stepped into the cab waiting at the front door. The car moved off immediately, but instead of my father what came to mind was the fresh face of that geisha in her Western hairstyle – and in particular her eyes.

Back at the hospital, I found my father eagerly awaiting my return. He sent everyone else outside the two-panel folding screen by the bed, and, gripping and caressing my hand, he began to talk about long-ago matters that I had never known – things from the time when he married my mother. They were inconsequential things – how he and she had gone to shop for a storage chest, or how they had eaten home-delivered sushi – but before I knew it my eyelids were growing hot inside, and down my father's wasted cheeks, too, tears were flowing.

My father died the next morning without a great deal of suffering. His mind seemed to grow confused before he died, and he would say things like 'Here comes a warship! Look at all the flags it has flying! Three cheers, everybody!' I don't remember his funeral at all. What I do remember is that when we transported his body from the hospital to his home, a great big spring moon was shining down on the hearse.

4

In mid-March of this year, when it was still cold enough for us to carry pocket warmers, my wife and I visited the cemetery for the first time in a long while – a very long while. Still, however, there was no change at all in either the small grave itself (of course) nor in the red pine stretching its branches above it.

The bones of all three people I have included in this 'Death Register' lie buried in the same corner of the cemetery in Yanaka – indeed, beneath the same gravestone. I recalled the time my mother's coffin was gently lowered into the grave. They must have done the same with Little Hatsu. In my father's case, though, I remember the gold teeth mixed in with the tiny white shards of bone at the crematorium.

I don't much like visiting the cemetery, and I would prefer to forget about my parents and sister if I could. On that particular day, though, perhaps because I was physically debilitated, I found myself staring at the blackened gravestone in the early spring afternoon sunlight and wondering which of the three had been the most fortunate.

A shimmering of heat –
Outside the grave
Alone I dwell.

Never before had I sensed these feelings of Jōsō's pressing in upon me with the force they truly had for me that day.

The Life of a Stupid Man

To my friend, Kume Masao:

I leave it to you to decide when and where to publish this manuscript – or whether to publish it at all.

You know most of the people who appear here, but if you do publish this, I don't want you adding an index identifying them.

I am living now in the unhappiest happiness imaginable. Yet, strangely, I have no regrets. I just feel sorry for anyone unfortunate enough to have had a bad husband, a bad son, a bad father like me. So goodbye, then. I have not tried – *consciously*, at least – to vindicate myself here.

Finally, I entrust this manuscript to you because I believe you probably know me better than anyone else. I may wear the skin of an urbane sophisticate, but in this manuscript I invite you to strip it off and laugh at my stupidity.

Akutagawa Ryūnosuke
20 June 1927

1. THE ERA

He was upstairs in a bookstore. Twenty years old at the time, he had climbed a ladder set against a bookcase and was searching for the newly-arrived Western books: Maupassant, Baudelaire, Strindberg, Ibsen, Shaw, Tolstoy . . .

The sun threatened to set before long, but he went on reading book spines with undiminished intensity. Lined up before him was not so much an array of books as the *fin de siècle* itself. Nietzsche, Verlaine, the Goncourt brothers, Dostoevsky, Hauptmann, Flaubert . . .

He took stock of their names as he struggled with the impending gloom. The books began to sink into the somber shadows. Finally his stamina gave out and he made ready to climb down. At that very moment, directly overhead, a single bare light bulb came on. Standing on his perch on top of the ladder, he looked down at the clerks and customers moving among the books. They were strangely small – and shabby.

Life is not worth a single line of Baudelaire.

He stood on the ladder, watching them below . . .

2. MOTHER

All the lunatics had been dressed in the same gray clothing, which seemed to give the large room an even more depressing look. One of them sat at an organ, playing a hymn over and over with great intensity. Another was dancing – or, rather, leaping about – in the very center of the room.

He stood watching this spectacle with a doctor of notably healthy complexion. Ten years earlier, his mother had been in no way different from these lunatics. In no way. And in fact in their smell he caught a whiff of his own mother's smell.

'Shall we go, then?'

The doctor led him down a corridor to another room. In a corner there were several brains soaking in large jars of alcohol. On one of the brains he noticed something faintly white, almost like a dollop of egg white. As he stood there chatting with the doctor, he thought again of his mother.

'The man who had this brain here was an engineer for the XX lighting company. He always thought of himself as a big shiny black dynamo.'

To avoid the doctor's eyes, he kept looking out the window. There was nothing out there but a brick wall topped with embedded broken bottles. It did, though, have thin growths of moss in dull white patches.

3. THE HOUSE

He was living in the upstairs room of a house in the suburbs. The second story tilted oddly because the ground was unstable.

In this room, his aunt would often quarrel with him, though not without occasional interventions from his adoptive parents. Still, he loved this aunt more than anyone. She never married, and by the time he was twenty, she was an old woman close to sixty.

He often wondered, in that suburban second story, if people who loved each other had to cause each other pain. Even as the thought crossed his mind, he was aware of the floor's eerie tilt.

4. TOKYO

A thick layer of cloud hung above the Sumida River. From the window of the little steamer, he watched the Mukōjima bank drawing closer. To his eyes, the blossoming cherry trees there looked as dreary as rags in a row. But almost before he knew it, in those trees – those cherry trees that had lined the bank of Mukōjima since the Edo Period – he was beginning to discover himself.

5. EGO

He and an elder colleague sat at a café table puffing on cigarettes. He said very little, but he paid close attention to his companion's every word.

'I spent half the day riding around in an automobile.'

'Was there something you needed to do?'

Cheek resting on his hand, the elder colleague replied with complete abandon, 'No, I just felt like riding around.'

The words released him into a world of which he knew nothing – a world of 'ego' close to the gods. He felt a kind of pain but, at the same time, a kind of joy.

The café was extremely small. Beneath a framed picture of the god Pan, however, a rubber tree in a red pot thrust its thick leaves out and down.

6. ILLNESS

In a steady ocean breeze, he spread out the large English dictionary and let his fingertip find words for him.

Talaria: A winged sandal.

Tale: A story.

Talipot: A coconut palm native to the East Indies. Trunk from 50 to 100 feet in height, leaves used for umbrellas, fans, hats, etc. Blooms once in 70 years . . .

His imagination painted a vivid picture of this bloom.

He then experienced an unfamiliar scratchy feeling in his throat, and before he knew it he had dropped a glob of phlegm on the dictionary. Phlegm? But it was not phlegm. He thought of the shortness of life and once again imagined the coconut blossom – the blossom of the coconut palm soaring on high far across the ocean.

7. PICTURE

It happened for him suddenly – quite suddenly. He was standing outside a bookstore, looking at a Van Gogh volume, when he suddenly understood what a 'picture' was. True, the Van Gogh was just a book of reproductions, but even in the photographs of those paintings, he sensed the vivid presence of nature.

This passion for pictures gave him a whole new way of looking at the world. He began to pay constant attention to the curve of a branch or the swell of a woman's cheek.

One rainy autumn evening, he was walking beneath an iron railroad bridge in the suburbs. Below the bank on the far side of the bridge stood a horse cart. As he passed it, he sensed that someone had come this way before. Someone? There was no need for him to wonder who that 'someone' might have been. In his twenty-three-year-old heart, a Dutchman with a cut ear and a long pipe in his mouth was fixing his gaze on this dreary landscape.

8. SPARKS: FLOWERS OF FIRE

Soaked by the rain, he trod along the asphalt. It was a heavy downpour. In the enveloping spray, he caught the smell of his rubberized coat.

Just then he saw the overhead trolley line giving off purple sparks and was strangely moved. His jacket pocket concealed the manuscript of the piece he was planning to publish in their little magazine. Walking through the rain, he looked back and up once again at the trolley line.

The cable was still sending sharp sparks into the air. He could think of nothing in life that he especially desired, but those purple sparks – those wildly-blooming flowers of fire – he would trade his life for the chance to hold them in his hands.

9. CADAVERS

A tag on a wire dangled from the big toe of each cadaver. The tags were inscribed with names, ages, and such. His friend bent over one corpse, peeling back the skin of its face with a deftly wielded scalpel. An expanse of beautiful yellow fat lay beneath the skin.

He studied the cadaver. He needed to do this to finish writing a story – a piece set against a Heian Period background – but he hated the stink of the corpses, which was like the smell of rotting apricots. Meanwhile, with wrinkled brow, his friend went on working his scalpel.

'You know, we're running out of cadavers these days,' his friend said.

His reply was ready: 'If *I* needed a corpse, I'd kill someone without the slightest malice.' Of course the reply stayed where it was – inside his heart.

10. THE MASTER

He was reading the Master's book beneath a great oak tree. Not a leaf stirred on the oak in the autumn sunlight. Far off in the sky, a scale with glass pans hung in perfect balance. He imagined such a vision as he read the Master's book . . .

11. DAWN

Night gradually gave way to dawn. He found himself on a street corner surveying a vast market. The swarming people and vehicles in the market were increasingly bathed in rose light.

He lit a cigarette and ambled into the market. Just then a lean black dog started barking at him, but he was not afraid. Indeed, he even loved this dog.

In the very center of the marketplace, a sycamore spread

its branches in all directions. He stood at the foot of the tree and looked up through the branches at the sky. A single star shone directly above him.

It was his twenty-fifth year – the third month after he first met the Master.

12. NAVAL PORT

Gloom filled the interior of the miniature submarine. Crouching down amid all the machinery, he peered into a small scope. What he saw there was a view of the bright naval port.

'You should be able to see the *Kongō*, too,' the naval officer explained to him.

As he was looking at the small warship through the square eyepiece, the thought of parsley popped into his mind for no reason – faintly aromatic parsley on top of a thirty-yen serving of beefsteak.

13. THE MASTER'S DEATH

In the wind after the rain, he walked down the platform of the new station. The sky was still dark. Across from the platform three or four railway laborers were swinging picks and singing loudly. The wind tore at the men's song and at his own emotions.

He left his cigarette unlit and felt a pain close to joy. 'Master near death,' read the telegram he had thrust into his coat pocket.

Just then the 6 a.m. Tokyo-bound train began to snake its way toward the station, rounding a pine-covered hill in the distance and trailing a wisp of smoke.

14. MARRIAGE

The day after he married her, he delivered a scolding to his wife: 'No sooner do you arrive here than you start wasting our money.' But the scolding was less from him than from his aunt, who had ordered him to deliver it. His wife apologized to him, of course, and to the aunt as well – with the potted jonquils she had bought for him in the room.

15. HE AND SHE

They led a peaceful life, surrounded by the garden's broad green *bashō* leaves.

It helped that their house was located in a town by the shore a full hour's train ride from Tokyo.

16. PILLOW

Pillowing his head on his rose-scented skepticism, he read a book by Anatole France. That even such a pillow might hold a god half-horse, he remained unaware.

17. BUTTERFLY

A butterfly fluttered its wings in a wind thick with the smell of seaweed. His dry lips felt the touch of the butterfly for the briefest instant, yet the wisp of wing dust still shone on his lips years later.

18. MOON

He happened to pass her on the stairway of a certain hotel. Her face seemed to be bathed in moonglow even now, in daylight. As he watched her walk on (they had never met), he felt a loneliness he had not known before.

19. MAN-MADE WINGS

He moved on from Anatole France to the eighteenth-century philosophers, though not to Rousseau. Perhaps this was because one side of him – the side easily moved by passion – was too close to Rousseau. Instead, he approached the author of *Candide*, who was closer to another side of him – the cool and richly intellectual side.

At twenty-nine, life no longer held any brightness for him, but Voltaire supplied him with man-made wings.

Spreading these man-made wings, he soared with ease into the sky. The higher he flew, the farther below him sank the joys and sorrows of a life bathed in the light of intellect. Dropping ironies and smiles upon the shabby towns below, he climbed through the open sky, straight for the sun – as if he had forgotten about that ancient Greek who plunged to his death in the ocean when his man-made wings were singed by the sun.

20. SHACKLES

He and his wife came to live with his adoptive parents when he went to work for a newspaper. He saw his contract, written on a single sheet of yellow paper, as a great source of strength. Later, however, he came to realize that the contract saddled *him* with all the obligations and the company with none.

21. CRAZY GIRL

Two rickshaws sped down a deserted country road beneath overcast skies. From the sea breeze it was clear that the road was headed toward the ocean. Puzzled that he felt not the slightest excitement about this rendezvous, he sat in the second rickshaw thinking about what had drawn him here. It was certainly not love. And if it was not love, then . . . but to avoid the conclusion, he had to tell himself, *At least we are in this as equals.*

The person riding in the front rickshaw was a crazy girl. And she was not alone in her madness: her younger sister had killed herself out of jealousy.

There's nothing I can do about this anymore.

He now felt a kind of loathing for this crazy girl – this woman who was all powerful animal instinct.

The two rickshaws soon passed a cemetery where the smell of the shore was strong. Several blackened, pagoda-shaped gravestones stood within the fence, which was woven of brushwood and decorated with oyster shells. He caught a glimpse of the ocean gleaming beyond the gravestones and suddenly – inexplicably – he felt contempt for the woman's husband for having failed to capture her heart.

22. A PAINTER

It was just a magazine illustration, but the ink drawing of a rooster showed a remarkable individuality. He asked a friend to tell him about the painter.

A week later, the painter himself came to pay him a visit. This was one of the most remarkable events in his entire life. He discovered in this painter a poetry of which no one else was aware. In addition, he discovered in himself a soul of which he himself had been unaware.

One chilly autumn evening, he was reminded of the painter by a stalk of corn: the way it stood there armed in its rough coat of leaves, exposing its delicate roots atop the mounded earth like so many nerves, it was also a portrait of his own most vulnerable self. The discovery only served to increase his melancholy.

It's too late now. But when the time comes . . .

23. THE WOMAN

From where he stood, the plaza was beginning to darken. He walked into the open space feeling slightly feverish. The electric lights in the windows of several large office buildings flashed against the clear, faintly silvery sky.

He halted at the curb and decided to wait for the woman there. Five minutes later she came walking toward him looking somewhat haggard. 'I'm exhausted,' she said with a smile when she caught sight of him. They walked through the fading light of the plaza side-by-side. This was their first time together. He felt ready to abandon anything and everything to be with her.

In the automobile she stared at him and asked, 'You're not going to regret this?'

'Not at all,' he answered with conviction.

She pressed her hand on his and said, 'I know *I* won't have any regrets.'

Again, as she said this, her face seemed to be bathed in moonlight.

24. THE BIRTH

He stood by the sliding screen, looking down at the midwife in her white surgical gown washing the baby. Whenever soap got in its eyes, the baby would wrinkle up its sad little face and let out a loud wail. It looked like a baby rat, and its odor stirred him to these irrepressible thoughts –

Why did this one have to be born – to come into the world like all the others, this world so full of suffering? Why did this one have to bear the destiny of having a father like me?

This was the first son his wife bore him.

25. STRINDBERG

He stood in the doorway, watching some grimy Chinese men playing Mahjongg in the moonlight where figs bloomed. Back in his room, he started reading *The Confessions of a Fool* beneath a squat lamp. He had barely read two pages when he caught himself with a sour smile. So – the lies that Strindberg wrote to his lover, the Countess, were hardly different from his own.

26. ANTIQUITY

He was nearly overwhelmed by peeling Buddhas, heavenly beings, horses and lotus blossoms. Looking up at them, he forgot everything – even his good fortune at having escaped the clutches of the crazy girl.

27. SPARTAN DISCIPLINE

He was walking down a back street with a friend when a hooded rickshaw came charging in their direction. He was surprised to recognize the passenger as the woman he had been with the night before. Her face seemed to be bathed in moonglow even now, in the daylight. With his friend present, they could not exchange even ordinary greetings.

'Pretty woman,' his friend said.

Eyes on the spring hills at the end of the street, he answered without the slightest hesitation:

'Yes, very.'

28. MURDER

The country road stank of cow manure in the sun. Mopping his sweat, he struggled up the steep hill. The ripened wheat on either side of the road gave off a pleasant scent.

'Kill him, kill him . . .'

Before he knew it, he was muttering this aloud to himself over and over. Kill whom? It was obvious to him. He recalled the cringing fellow with close-cropped hair.

Just then, the domed roof of a Catholic church appeared beyond the yellow wheat.

29. FORM

It was a cast-iron saké bottle. With its finely incised lines, it had managed at some point to teach him the beauty of 'form'.

30. RAIN

In the big bed he talked with her about many things. Beyond the bedroom window it was raining. The blossoms of the crinum tree had begun to rot in the rain, it seemed. Her face, as always, looked as if it were in moonlight, yet talking with her was not entirely free of boredom. He lay on his stomach, had himself a quiet smoke, and realized he had now been with her for seven years.

Do I still love this woman? he asked himself. He was in the habit of observing himself so closely that the answer came as a surprise to him: *I do*.

31. THE GREAT EARTHQUAKE

The odor was something close to overripe apricots. Catching a hint of it as he walked through the charred ruins, he found himself thinking such thoughts as these: *The smell of corpses rotting in the sun is not as bad as I would have expected*. When he stood before a pond where bodies were piled upon bodies, however, he discovered that the old Chinese expression, 'burning the nose', was no mere sensory exaggeration of grief and horror. What especially moved him was the corpse of a child of twelve or thirteen. He felt something like envy as he looked at it, recalling such expressions as 'Those whom the gods love die young.' Both his sister and his half-brother had lost their houses to fire. His sister's husband, though, was on a suspended sentence for perjury.

Too bad we didn't all die.

Standing in the charred ruins, he could hardly keep from feeling this way.

32. FIGHT

He had a quarrel with his half-brother that ended in a physical brawl. True, he was a constant source of pressure for this younger brother, who in turn cost him a good deal of freedom. Relatives were always telling the young man, 'be like your brother', but for him, this was like being bound hand and foot. Locked in each other's grip, they fell near the edge of the veranda. He still remembers the one crape myrtle bush in the garden by the veranda – its load of brilliant red blossoms beneath a sky about to drop its rainy burden.

33. HERO

From the window of Voltaire's house, he found himself looking up toward a high mountain. There was nothing to be seen on the glacier-topped mountain, not even a vulture. There was, however, a short Russian man doggedly climbing the trail.

After night fell, beneath the bright lamp in Voltaire's house, he wrote this didactic poem (still picturing that Russian man climbing the mountain).

> You who more than anyone obeyed the Ten
>   Commandments
> Are you who more than anyone broke the Ten
>   Commandments.
>
> You who more than anyone loved the masses
> Are you who more than anyone despised the masses.
>
> You who more than anyone burned with ideals
> Are you who more than anyone knew reality.
>
> You are what our Eastern world has bred –
> An electric locomotive that smells of flowering
>   grasses.

34. COLOR

At thirty he found himself loving a piece of vacant land. It contained only some moss and scattered bits of brick and tile. To his eyes, however, it was exactly like a Cezanne landscape.

He suddenly recalled his passions of seven or eight years earlier. And when he did so, he realized that seven or eight years earlier he had known nothing about color.

35. COMIC PUPPET

He wanted to live life so intensely that he could die at any moment without regrets. But still, out of deference to his adoptive parents and his aunt, he kept himself in check. This created both light and dark sides to his life. Seeing a comic puppet in a Western tailor's shop made him wonder how close he himself was to such a figure. His self beyond consciousness, however – his 'second self' – had long since put such feelings into a story.

36. TEDIUM

He was walking through a field of plume grass with a university student. 'You fellows still have a strong will to live, I suppose?'

'Yes, of course, but you, too . . .'

'Not any more,' he said. He was telling the truth. At some point he had lost interest in life. 'I *do* have the will to create, though.'

'But surely the will to create is a form of the will to live . . . ?'

To this he did not reply. Above the field's red plumes rose the sharp outline of an active volcano. He viewed the peak with something close to envy, though he had no idea why this was so . . .

37. 'WOMAN OF HOKURIKU'

He met a woman he could grapple with intellectually. He barely extricated himself from the crisis by writing a number of lyric poems, some under the title 'Woman of Hokuriku'. These conveyed a sense of heartbreak as when one knocks away a brilliant coating of snow frozen onto a tree trunk.

> Hat of sedge dancing in the wind:
> How could it fail to drop into the road?
> What need I fear for my name?
> For your name alone do I fear.

38. PUNISHMENT

They were on the balcony of a hotel surrounded by trees in bud. He was drawing pictures to amuse a little boy – the only son of the crazy girl, with whom he had broken off relations seven years earlier.

The crazy girl lit a cigarette and watched them play. With an oppressive feeling, he went on drawing trains and airplanes. Fortunately, the boy was not his, but it still pained him greatly when the child called him 'uncle'.

After the boy wandered off, the crazy girl, still smoking her cigarette, said suggestively:

'Don't you think he looks like you?'

'Not at all. Besides –'

'But you do know about "prenatal influence", I'm sure.'

He looked away from her in silence, but in his heart he wanted to strangle her.

39. MIRRORS

He was in the corner of a café, chatting with a friend. The friend was eating a baked apple and talking about the recent cold weather when he himself began to sense a certain contradiction in the conversation.

'Hey, wait a minute – you're still a bachelor, right?'

'Not exactly: I'm getting married next month.'

That silenced him. The mirrors set in the café walls reflected him in endless numbers. Coldly. Menacingly.

40. DIALOGUE

Why do you attack the present social system?

Because I see the evils that capitalism has engendered.

Evils? I thought you recognized no difference between good and evil. How do you make a living, then?

He engaged thus in dialogue with an angel – an angel in an impeccable top hat.

41. ILLNESS

He suffered an onslaught of insomnia. His physical strength began to fade as well. The doctors gave him various diagnoses – gastric hyperacidity, gastric atony, dry pleurisy, neurasthenia, chronic conjunctivitis, brain fatigue . . .

But he knew well enough what was wrong with him: he was ashamed of himself and afraid of *them* – afraid of the society he so despised.

One afternoon when snow clouds hung over the city, he was in the corner of a café, smoking a cigar and listening to music from the gramophone on the other side of the room. He found the music permeating his emotions in a strange new way. When it ended, he walked over to the gramophone to read the label on the record.

'Magic Flute – Mozart.'

All at once it became clear to him: Mozart too had broken the Ten Commandments and suffered. Probably not the way *he* had, but . . .

He bowed his head and returned to his table in silence.

42. THE LAUGHTER OF THE GODS

At thirty-five, he was walking through a pinewood with the spring sun beating down on it. He was recalling, too, the words he had written a few years earlier: 'It is unfortunate for the gods that, unlike us, they cannot commit suicide.'

43. NIGHT

Night closed in again. The rough sea sent up spray in the fading light. Beneath these skies, he married his wife anew. This brought them joy, but there was suffering as well. With them, their three sons watched the lightning over the open sea. His wife, holding one of the boys in her arms, seemed to be fighting back tears.

'See the boat over there?' he asked her.

'Yes . . .'

'That boat with the mast cracked in two . . .'

44. DEATH

Taking advantage of his sleeping alone, he tried to hang himself with a sash tied over the window lattice. When he slipped his head into the sash, however, he suddenly became afraid of death. Not that he feared the suffering he would have to experience at the moment of dying. He decided to try it again, using his pocket watch to see how long it would take. This time, everything began to cloud over after a short interval of pain. He was sure that once he got past that, he would enter death. Checking the hands of his watch, he discovered that the pain lasted one minute and twenty-some seconds. It was pitch dark outside the lattices, but the wild clucking of chickens echoed in the darkness.

45. DIVAN

Divan was giving him new inner power. This was an 'Oriental Goethe' he had not known before. He saw the author standing with quiet confidence on the Other Shore, far beyond good and evil, and he felt an envy close to despair. In his eyes, the poet Goethe was even greater than the poet Christ. For in the heart of the poet Goethe, there bloomed not only the roses of the Acropolis and Golgotha but the rose of Arabia as well. If only he had the least ability to follow in this poet's footsteps!

Once he had finished reading *Divan* and recovered somewhat from its terrifying emotional impact, he could only despise himself for having been born such a eunuch in life!

46. LIES

He felt the suicide of his sister's husband as a terrible blow. Now he was responsible for his sister's family as well. To him at least, his future looked as gloomy as the end of the day. He felt something like a sneer for his own spiritual bankruptcy (he was aware of all of his faults and weak points, every single one of them), but he went on reading one book after another. Even Rousseau's *Confessions*, though, was full of the most heroic lies. And when it came to Tōson's *New Life*, he felt he had never met such a cunning hypocrite as that novel's protagonist. The one who truly moved him, though, was François Villon. He found in that poet's many works the 'beautiful male'.

Sometimes in his dreams the image would come to him of Villon waiting to be hanged. Like Villon, he had several times nearly fallen to the ultimate depths of life, but neither his situation nor his physical energy would permit him to keep this up. He grew gradually weaker, like the tree Swift saw so long ago, withering from the top down.

47. PLAYING WITH FIRE

She had a radiant face, like the morning sun on a thin sheet of ice. He was fond of her, but he did not love her, nor had he ever laid a finger on her.

'I've heard you want to die,' she said.

'Yes – or rather, it's not so much that I want to die as that I'm tired of living.'

This dialogue led to a vow to die together.

'It would be a Platonic suicide, I suppose,' she said.

'A Platonic double suicide.'

He was amazed at his own sangfroid.

48. DEATH

He did not die with her, but he took a certain satisfaction in his never having touched her. She often spoke with him as though their dialogue had never happened. She did once give him a bottle of cyanide with the remark, 'As long as we have this, it will give us both strength.'

And it did indeed give him strength. Sitting in a rattan chair, observing the new growth of a *shii* tree, he often thought of the peace that death would give him.

49. STUFFED SWAN

With the last of his strength, he tried to write his autobiography, but it did not come together as easily as he had hoped. This was because of his remaining pride and skepticism, and a calculation of what was in his own best interest. He couldn't help despising these qualities in himself; but neither could he help feeling that 'Everyone is the same under the skin.' He tended to think that Goethe's title 'Poetry and Truth' could serve for anyone's autobiography, but he knew that not everyone is moved by literature. His own works were unlikely to appeal to people who were not like him and had not lived a life like his – this was another feeling that worked upon him. And so he decided to write his own brief 'Poetry and Truth'.

Once he had finished writing 'The Life of a Stupid Man', he happened to see a stuffed swan in a secondhand shop. It stood with its head held high, but its wings were yellowed and moth-eaten. As he thought about his life, he felt both tears and mockery welling up inside him. All that lay before him was madness or suicide. He walked down the darkening street alone, determined now to wait for the destiny that would come to annihilate him.

50. CAPTIVE

One of his friends went mad. He had always felt close to this man because he understood far more deeply than anyone else the loneliness that lurked beneath his jaunty mask. He visited him a few times after the madness struck.

'You and I are both possessed by a demon,' the friend whispered, 'the demon of the *fin de siècle*.'

Two or three days later, he heard, the man ate roses on the way to a hot-spring resort. When the friend was hospitalized, he recalled once sending him a terra cotta piece. It was a bust of the author of *The Inspector General*, one of the friend's favorite writers. Thinking how Gogol, too, had gone mad, he could not help feeling that there was a force governing all of them.

Just as he reached the point of utter exhaustion, he happened to read Raymond Radiguet's dying words, 'God's soldiers are coming to get me,' and sensed once again the laughter of the gods. He tried to fight against his own superstitions and sentimentalism, but he was physically incapable of putting up any kind of struggle. The 'demon of the *fin de siècle*' was preying on him without a doubt. He envied medieval men's ability to find strength in God. But for him, believing in God – in God's love – was an impossibility, though even Cocteau had done it!

51. DEFEAT

The hand with the pen began to tremble, and before long he was even drooling. The only time his head ever cleared was after a sleep induced by eight-tenths of a gram of Veronal, and even then it never lasted more than thirty minutes or an hour. He barely made it through each day in the gloom, leaning as it were upon a chipped and narrow sword.

PENGUIN

LITTLE BLACK

CLASSICS

“人生诚然是如
过眼浮云。
哎呀呀，
我简直不知道
怎么说才好，
多么可怜！”

PENGUIN

LITTLE BLACK

CLASSICS

*此中文译本译自日语原文

傻子的一生

The Life of a Stupid Man

[日] 芥川龙之介 著

文洁若 译

中信出版集团 · 北京

图书在版编目（CIP）数据

企鹅经典 · 小黑书 . 第一辑 : 英、汉 / (日) 吉田兼好等著 ; 文东等译 . -- 北京 : 中信出版社 , 2018.11 (2022.7 重印)
书名原文 : Penguin Little Black Classics
ISBN 978-7-5086-9400-9

Ⅰ . ①企… Ⅱ . ①吉… ②文… Ⅲ . ①世界文学一作品综合集一英、汉 Ⅳ . ① I11

中国版本图书馆 CIP 数据核字 (2018) 第 193780 号

企鹅经典：小黑书　第一辑
傻子的一生

著　　者：[日] 芥川龙之介
译　　者：文洁若
出版发行：中信出版集团股份有限公司
（北京市朝阳区惠新东街甲 4 号富盛大厦 2 座 邮编 100029）
承 印 者：河北鹏润印刷有限公司

开　　本：787mm×1092mm　1/32　　印　　张：41　　字　　数：300 千字
版　　次：2018 年 11 月第 1 版　　印　　次：2022 年 7 月第13次印刷
京权图字：01-2018-6477
书　　号：ISBN 978-7-5086-9400-9
定　　价：149.00 元（全 10 册）

目录

竹林中

樵夫答典史问

是啊，发现那具尸体的正是我。今天早晨，我跟往常一样去砍伐后山的杉树。没料到山后的竹林里，竟有这么一具尸体。地点在哪儿？离山科的驿路有那么四五町[1]光景。竹子当中夹杂着细小的杉树，那地方连个人影儿也没有。

尸体上身穿淡蓝色短褂，头上戴着有皱纹的京式乌帽，脸朝天倒在那里。想想看，这一刀刚好戳在胸口上，

1. 町是日本长度单位，一町约合 109 米。（说明：书中脚注均为译者注。）

尸体周围竹子的落叶简直就像是浸透了苏枋[1]水般地染红了。不，已经不再流血了，伤口好像早就凝固了。那里一只马蝇紧紧地叮在伤口上，似乎连我的脚步声都没理会。

没有看见什么凶器吗？没有，啥都没有。只是旁边的杉树底下丢着一根绳子。另外——对，除了绳子还有一把梳子。尸体旁边只有这两样东西。可是周围的草和竹叶给踩得很厉害，看来那个汉子被害以前，还曾拼命搏斗过一番。什么，有马没有？那里根本进不去马，竹林后面的路才能够走马呢！

云游僧答典史问

不错，昨天我碰见过那个如今成了尸体的汉子。昨天晌午，地点是从关山到山科的路上。那个人跟着一个骑马的妇女朝关山这边走来。女人遮着面纱，我看不见她的脸，只看见了她身上那件夹衣的颜色——好像是红面蓝里子。马是桃花马，记得马鬃是剃光了的[2]。马有

1. 苏枋，也叫苏木、苏方，是一种常绿小乔木，心材浸液可做红色染料。

2. 原文为剃有法师发的马，即将马鬃像和尚头那样剃光。

多高吗？总有四尺四寸吧。……不过我是沙门，不大懂得这种事。那个男子——不，既佩着大刀，也带着弓箭，而且在上了黑漆的箭囊里插着二十来支箭，这我至今还清清楚楚地记得。

我做梦也想不到那个汉子会落到这么个下场。人生诚然是如过眼浮云。哎呀呀，我简直不知道怎么说才好，多么可怜！

捕役[1]答典史问

我抓到的那个人吗？他确实是个臭名昭著的强盗，名叫多襄丸。不过我逮他的时候，他正在粟田口的石桥上嗯嗯地呻吟着呢，大概是从马上摔下来的吧。时间吗？是昨天晚上初更光景。上回我差点捉住了他，被他逃掉了。那一回他穿的也是藏青短褂，腰里插着大刀。您瞧，如今他除了刀以外，还带着弓箭呢。啊？原来那个被害的人携带的也是这些……那么杀人的无疑就是这个多襄丸了。缠着皮的弓，黑漆的箭囊，鹰翎的箭十七

1.原文为放免一词，即日本古代对一些犯人免除徒刑，利用他们来追捕罪犯。

支——这都是那个被害人随身带的吧。对，正如您说的，马也正是那匹剃光了鬃毛的桃花马。准是因果报应，被这畜生甩下来啦。它就在石桥过去一点儿的地方，拖着长长的缰绳，在吃路旁的青芒呢。

在洛中出没的强盗当中，多襄丸这家伙也是个好色之徒。去年秋天，有个好像是来进香的妇女和丫头一道在鸟部寺宝头卢的后山被杀，据说就是这家伙干的。男的被他杀了，骑桃花马的那个女人也不知道给带到什么地方去，后来怎样了呢。也许我不该多嘴，这一点也请您调查一下吧。

老媪答典史问

没错，这就是我闺女嫁的那个男人的尸体。他不是京城的人，是若狭国府的武士。名字叫金泽武弘，二十六岁。不，他性情温和，绝不会招人忌恨的。

女儿吗？女儿叫真砂，今年十九岁。她性格刚强，几乎赛过男子。除了武弘以外，她不曾跟别的男人好过。小小的瓜子儿脸，肤色微黑，左眼角上有颗痣。

武弘昨天跟我女儿一道动身到若狭去，竟出了这样

的事，真不知前世造了什么孽！女婿已然这样，也只好认命了，可我女儿怎样了呢？真把我急坏了。我这苦老婆子求求您啦，一辈子也忘不了您，哪怕上天入地，也恳求您务必找到我女儿的下落。不管怎么说，可恨的是那个叫作什么多襄丸的强盗。他不但害了我女婿，连我女儿也……（老媪泣不成声）

多襄丸的供词

那个男人是我杀死的，可我没杀女的。她到哪儿去啦？这我可不知道。喏，慢着。再怎么拷问，不知道的也说不出来呀！而且事到如今，我不打算卑鄙地隐瞒什么了。

昨天刚过晌午，我碰见了那对夫妇。那时候碰巧刮了一阵风，撩起了那女人长长垂下的面纱，我瞅见了她的脸。可一眨眼的工夫，就又看不见了。一方面也是由于这个缘故吧，我只觉得那个女人长得像菩萨一样标致。我一时打定了主意，即使杀了那个男的，也非把女的抢到手不可。

咳，杀死个把男人，并不是像你们想的那样了不起

的事。要抢女人，男人横竖是要给杀死的。只不过我杀人是用腰间佩的大刀，而你们杀人不用刀，单凭权力，凭金钱，往往还仅仅凭了那张伪善的嘴巴就够了。不错，血是不会流的，人还活得好好的——然而还是给杀了。想想有多么罪孽呀！谁知道究竟是你们坏还是我坏呢？（嘲讽的微笑）

不过，要是能够不杀男人就把女人抢到手，倒也没什么不好。哦，那时候原是想尽量避免杀男人而把女人抢到手的。但在那山科的驿路上，说什么也办不到。所以我就想方设法把那对夫妇引到山里去。

这也不费什么事。我跟那对夫妇搭伴走，跟他们说，对面山上有个古冢，我一挖，挖出了许许多多镜子和大刀，我悄悄地给埋在山后的竹林里了。谁要是想买，随便哪样，出几个钱就成。那个男的听了我这话，不知不觉地动了心——您瞧，贪欲有多么可怕啊。不到半个时辰，那对夫妇就跟我一道走上了山路。

到了竹林前面我就说，宝贝埋在这里呢，来看吧。男的利欲熏心，自然同意。可是那个女人连马都没下，说是就在那儿等着。看到竹林那么密，也就难怪她会这么说了。说实在的，这正合我意，就把女人留在那儿，

跟男的一块儿走进了竹林。

竹林里起初净是竹子。走了十六七丈，才是一簇疏疏朗朗的杉树——为了达到我的目的，没有比这地方更便当的了。我扒开竹枝，撒了个听起来好像很有道理的谎，说宝贝就埋在杉树底下。听我这么一说，男的就拼命朝着透过竹叶已经能够看到细小杉树的那个方向走去。这当儿竹子稀疏起来，并立着好几棵杉树——刚走到这儿，我就马上把对方按倒。那人不愧是个佩刀的，好像相当有力气。无奈我给他个措手不及，他怎么也招架不住，马上就给捆到一棵杉树脚下了。绳子吗？这是做贼的妙处，随时得翻墙越壁，所以腰间早就准备好了。当然，为了不让他喊出声来，就用竹子的落叶堵上他的嘴，此外就没什么麻烦了。

我把男的安排停当后，就又到女人那里去说，那个男的好像得了急病，要她快去看看。不用说，这一次也达到了目的。女的已经摘掉那个垂着面纱的市女笠，就那样被我拉着手走到竹林深处来了。到这儿一看，男的给捆在杉树脚上呢——女人一看到这幅情景，不知什么工夫从怀里掏出了小刀，闪亮亮地拔出了鞘。我从来还没见过那么烈性子的女人呢。这当儿只要稍微一大意，

就会被她一刀戳破了肚皮。不，即使躲过了这一下，在她的乱刀下面，指不定会受什么样的伤呢。我毕竟是多襄丸啊，好歹连大刀也没拔，到底把她的小刀打落了。再怎么刚强的女人，没有了武器也就没办法了。我终于照原来想的那样，不杀害男人，就把女人弄到了手。

不杀害男人——是的，只要把女人弄到手，我并不曾打算要男人的命。可是正当我丢下伏在地上哭泣的女人，往竹林外头逃去的时候，那个女人突然像疯子一样抓住了我的胳膊，而且她断断续续地喊道，你也罢，我丈夫也罢，你们之间总得死一个。在两个男人面前丢丑，比死还痛苦。后来还气喘吁吁地说，不管是你们哪个活下来，我就情愿跟他。这时我猛地对那个男人动了杀机。（阴郁的兴奋）

我这么一说，你们一定会认为我比你们还要残酷。那是因为你们不曾看见那个女人的脸，尤其是一瞬间她那烈火般的眸子。我和这个女人眼光相遇时，心想就是天打雷劈，也要把她娶到手。我只有娶她为妻这么一个念头。这不是像你们所想象的那种下流的色欲。假若当时除了色欲之外什么愿望也没有，我就是把女人踢倒了，也非逃跑不可。这样，我的大刀也就不至

于沾上男人的血了。但是我在阴暗的竹林中定睛看了看女人的脸。当时我就打定主意，不杀死男人，绝不离开这里。

但是杀男人嘛，我也不想用卑鄙的手段。我给他松了绑，要求跟他用大刀来决斗。（丢在杉树脚下的绳子，就是那时忘了扔掉的）那个男人依然煞白着脸，马上把大刀拔出了鞘。一眨眼的工夫，一声不响气冲冲地向我扑来——交手的结果怎样，那就不用多说了。第二十三个回合，我的大刀把对方的胸膛刺透了。请不要忘记——是第二十三个回合啊。直到现在，我对他这一点还是佩服的。因为他是天下唯一和我交手到二十回合以上的。（快活的微笑）

男人刚一倒下，我就提着血淋淋的大刀，回头去看女人。可哪里想到，女人已经无影无踪了。她逃到哪儿去了呢？我在那簇杉树中找了找，可是竹子的落叶上，连点可疑的痕迹也没有。竖起耳朵听了听，只传来了男子喉间发出的断气声。

也许我刚开始抡刀的时候，那个女人为了呼救，就钻出竹林逃跑了——想到这里，这下子我为了保全自己的性命，就拿了大刀和弓箭，立即又回到原来的山路上

去。女人的马还在那儿静静地吃草呢。以后的事情就用不着去说了。只是在进京之前，我已经把大刀卖掉了——我的口供完啦。我这颗脑袋总有挂在苦楝树梢[1]上的一天，请处我以极刑吧。（气概昂然）

来到清水寺的女人的忏悔

那个穿藏青短褂的人把我污辱以后，就瞧着我那被绑起来的丈夫嘲笑起来。我丈夫该是多么气愤啊。可他不管怎么挣扎，浑身绑着的绳子只是越勒越紧。我不由得滚也似的跑到丈夫身边去——不，是想要跑过去。可是那个人马上一脚把我踢倒了。就在这当儿，我觉察到丈夫眼里有一种难以形容的光。难以形容的——直到现在，我一想起他那眼神还不禁发抖。丈夫一句话也说不出来，在这一刹那间，用眼睛把他整个儿的心意传给我了。可闪烁在他眼睛里的，既不是愤怒也不是悲哀——只是蔑视我的冷冰冰的光呀！与其说是被那个人踢的，毋宁说是由于受了这眼光的刺激，我不由得喊了一句什

1. 日本古代在牢狱门口植以苦楝树，以便将犯人枭首示众。

么，就终于昏倒了。

后来我总算恢复了知觉。一看，那个穿藏青短褂的人已经不知去向。只剩下我丈夫被绑在杉树脚下。我从落满竹叶的地上勉勉强强撑起身来，看了看丈夫的脸。但是丈夫的眼神跟方才丝毫没有两样。在冷冰冰的轻蔑之下，蕴藏着憎恶的光。羞耻，悲哀，愤怒——简直不知道怎么形容当时我心里的感觉才好。我摇摇晃晃地站起来，走到丈夫身边。

“你呀，事情已经是这样了，我再也不能跟你在一块儿啦。我打算一死了之。可是……可是请你也死掉。你看到了我的耻辱，我不能让你一个人就这样活下去。”

我拼命地说了这么几句。然而丈夫只是厌恶地盯着我。我按捺住几乎要破裂的胸膛，搜寻丈夫的大刀。大概是给强盗抢去了，大刀自不用说，竹丛里连弓箭也没有了。可是幸亏小刀还掉在我脚底下。我举起小刀，又对丈夫说了一遍：“那么，请允许我先要了你的命，我随后就来。”

丈夫听了我这话，好容易才动了动嘴唇。他嘴里塞满了竹子的落叶，声音当然是一点也听不见的。但是我一看见他的嘴动，马上就明白了他在说什么。他依然对

我抱着轻蔑的态度，说了句:“杀吧。”我几乎像做梦一般朝着丈夫那穿着淡蓝色短褂的胸口扑哧一声把小刀戳了进去。

我这时大概又昏过去了。好歹恢复知觉后，四下里打量了一下，丈夫仍旧绑在那里，早已咽了气。透过交错的竹子和杉树，一道夕阳从天空里射到他那苍白的脸上。我忍着哭声，给尸体松了绑。于是……于是我怎样了呢？唯独这一点，我已经没有力气来说明了。横竖我怎样也没有能耐去死。把小刀往喉咙里戳也罢，投身到山脚下的池子里也罢，种种办法都试过了，可就是死不了。现在还这么活着，这也不是什么光彩的事。（淡淡的惨笑）像我这样没有骨气的人，说不定连大慈大悲的观音菩萨也不屑睬一眼了。可是，杀了丈夫的我，被强盗糟蹋了的我，究竟该怎么办才好呢？我究竟……我……（突然激烈地抽搭）

鬼魂借巫女之口所说的话

——强盗奸污完了我的妻子，就在那儿坐下来，用种种话来安慰她。我当然说不出话来，身子也给绑在杉

树脚下，可是我多次给妻子使眼色，想暗示她，不要把这个人的话信以为真。要知道，不管他说什么都是一派谎言。可是我妻子沮丧地坐在竹子的落叶上，一个劲儿地望着自己的膝头。怎么看也像是在专心听强盗的话哪。我嫉妒得浑身发抖，可是强盗花言巧语地变着法儿讲下去，最后竟大胆地说出了这样的话：即便就被糟蹋这么一回，反正跟丈夫也很难再圆满相处了。与其跟这样的丈夫过下去，你有没有做我妻子的打算呢？我正因为疼你，才干出了这样一桩无法无天的事来。

听强盗这么一说，妻子竟然就心荡神驰地仰起脸来。我还从来没看到妻子像那个时刻那么美丽过。可是那个美丽的妻子，当着像这样被绑起来的我的面，怎么回答了强盗呢？尽管魂游冥世，每逢想起妻子的回答，就怒火中烧。妻子确实是这样说的：“那么，请你随便把我带到哪儿去吧。”（沉默良久）

妻子的罪过，还不止于此。要仅仅是这样，我也不至于在冥冥之中这么痛苦了。可是妻子犹如做梦一般被强盗牵着手往竹林外面走去的当儿，脸色忽然变得刷白，指着杉树脚下的我，像发了疯般地喊了好几遍：“请你把那个人杀掉。只要他活着，我就不能跟你在一块

儿。”“请你把那个人杀掉”——这句话像一股狂风，即使现在也好像要把我头朝下刮落到遥远、黑暗的深渊底下去。哪怕是一次，难道人的嘴巴曾吐出过这样可憎恶的话吗？哪怕是一次，难道人的耳朵曾听到过这样可诅咒的话吗？哪怕是一次，难道……（突然一阵冷笑）听了这话，连强盗也煞白了脸。“请你把那个人杀掉。”妻子边这么喊着，边拉住强盗的胳膊。强盗定睛看着我的妻子，不说杀也不说不杀……我刚这么一想，妻子一脚就给踢倒在竹子的落叶上了。（又迸发出一阵冷笑）强盗安详地抱起胳膊，向我看了看：“那个女人你打算怎么处置？是杀掉，还是饶她一条命？点一下头吧：杀掉吗？”——单凭这句话，我就想赦免强盗的罪孽。（再度沉默良久）

趁着我迟疑的工夫，妻子喊叫了一句什么，立即逃到竹林深处去了。强盗马上扑奔过去，可是好像连袖子也没抓着。我仿佛是在梦幻中看到了这幅情景。

妻子逃掉以后，强盗夺过我的大刀弓箭，把我身上绑的绳子割断一处。我记得强盗消失在竹林外面的时候，喃喃地说了句：“这回该轮到我了。”以后，周围寂静下来。不，还有什么人的哭声哩。我一边解开绳子，一边

侧耳细听。呃，这不是我自己的哭声吗？（第三次沉默良久）

我很吃力地从杉树脚下抬起我那精疲力竭的身子。妻子落下的小刀就在我跟前闪着光。我把它拿在手里，朝着胸口一戳。一块带着腥味的玩意儿涌到嘴里来。我丝毫不觉得痛苦，只是胸口凉了以后，四下里越发寂然无声。哎呀，多么凄凉啊！连只小鸟也不飞到这山后的竹林上空来啁啾，唯有几抹阳光寂寥地飘在竹子和杉树梢头。就连这阳光也逐渐暗淡下来，杉树和竹子都再也看不见了。我倒在那儿，笼罩在深沉的静穆之中。

这当儿有谁蹑手蹑脚地走到我身边来了。我想掉过头去看一看，但是不知什么时候我周围已经昏暗下来了。什么人——不知是谁，用看不见的手悄悄地拔掉了我胸口上的小刀。同时，鲜血又涌到我嘴里来。从此，我就永远沉沦在冥世的黑暗中了……

一九二一年十二月

（文洁若　译）

点鬼簿

一

我母亲是个狂人。我从未对母亲有过骨肉之情。我母亲用梳子把头发卷在头顶上，总是独自坐在位于芝[1]的娘家，咕噜咕噜地吸烟袋[2]。她的脸小，身体也小。不知为什么，那张脸是灰色的，没有朝气。我曾经读过《西厢记》，读到“土气息，泥滋味”一语时，一下就想起了我母亲那张脸——消瘦的侧脸。

---

1. 芝是东京都港区的一个街区。
2. 烟袋是一种吸烟用具，一般在细竹管的一端安着烟袋锅儿，可以装烟，另一端安着玉石、翡翠等制成的嘴儿，可以衔在嘴里吸。

说这番话的我，从未被母亲照料过。有一次，养母带着我，特意到楼上去问候母亲，她竟然冷不防用烟袋打了我的脑袋。我对此事记忆犹新。不过，总的来说，我母亲是一位实在文静的狂人。我或我的姐姐迫使她画画的时候，她就在折成四折的日本纸[1]上为我们画。非但用墨笔画，还把我姐姐的水彩画颜料涂在她自己所画男男女女的衣服啦、草木和花上面。只不过这些画上的人物个个都长着活脱儿是狐狸的脸。

我十一岁那一年的秋天，我母亲去世了。与其说是生病而死，毋宁说是衰弱而死的吧。唯独她逝世前前后后的记忆却比较清晰地留在我的记忆里。

大概是由于接到了病笃的电报吧。在一个无风的深夜，我和养母同乘一辆人力车，从本所[2]赶到芝。迄今我还没使用过叫作围巾的玩意儿。然而，特别在这个夜晚，我记得围了一条画了南画[3]里一些山水风景的薄绸

---

1. 原文为“半纸”，习字、写信用的日本纸，长 24 厘米，宽 34 厘米左右。

2. 本所是东京都墨田区的一个街区。

3. 南画也叫文人画。是 18、19 世纪很多日本画家采用的一种绘画风格。在江户中期和后期，一些具有独特创作能力的画家属于这一画派。其画风是依据 17 至 18 世纪具有个性的中国清代绘画形成的。同时，南画画家们在构图及笔法上改变了中国文人画的夸张手法，作品中常带有一种幽默感。

手绢儿。也记得那条手绢儿发出的叫作“蝴蝶花”的香水气味。

我母亲躺在二楼下方那间八榻榻米[1]的客厅里。我和比我大四岁的姐姐跪在母亲的枕畔，两个人都不断地号啕大哭。尤其是有人在我后边念诵“驾鹤西去，驾鹤西去”，当时我越发感到悲伤不禁涌上心头。然而，一直闭着眼睛、几乎是死者的母亲突然睁开双目，说了些话。我们尽管凄怆，却小声哧哧地笑起来了。

次日晚上，我依然在母亲的枕边坐到将近拂晓。不过，不知为何，这一晚我一滴眼泪也流不出来。我在几乎不停地嚎哭的姐姐面前觉得丢脸，于是拼命地假装哭泣。同时，我又相信既然自己哭不出来，母亲必定不会死。

第三天的夜晚，我母亲几乎没怎么痛苦就咽了气。死前大概清醒过来了，凝视着我们的面孔，扑簌簌地落泪。不过，依然像平素那样什么话也不说。

入殓之后，我也不禁经常哭泣。有一位叫作“王子[2]的姑妈”的远亲说：“实在使人钦佩。”我当时唯一的想

1. 也称“叠”“帖”，榻榻米为音译，指铺在和式房间地板上的草垫子，呈长方形，尺寸大小各地不尽相同。一般宽90厘米，长180厘米，厚约6厘米。

2. 东京都北区内的一个街区。

法就是，她是那种对玄妙的事感到钦佩的人。

我母亲出殡的那一天，姐姐拿着灵牌，我跟在后边，拿着香炉。两个人都是乘人力车去的。我有时打盹儿，总会在险些要把香炉掉下去的时候，突然惊醒。一直就这样，我们好像永远也到不了谷中[1]似的。相当长的送葬行列静悄悄地沿着秋季那总是晴朗的东京的大街前进。

我母亲的忌辰是十一月二十八日，戒名是“归命院妙成日进大师”。可是二十年后，我却不记得自己的亲生父亲的忌辰与戒名。多半是因为对十一岁的我而言，记住忌辰与戒名也是值得夸耀的一件事吧。

二

我有一位姐姐。尽管她身体多病，却成了两个孩子的母亲。想添加在我《点鬼簿》中的，当然不是这位姐姐的事，而是那位恰好在我出生前，突然夭折了的姐姐的事。据说，我们三姐弟中，她最聪明。

1. 东京都台东区内的一个街区。

这位姐姐叫作初子，或许是由于她生为长女。我家的佛盒上至今有一张“小初”的相片，装在小小的镜框里。“小初”一点也不像是衰弱的孩子。长着小酒窝儿的两颊，就像熟杏子一般，圆溜溜的……

被父母过多地宠爱的终究是“小初”。他们把“小初”从芝的新钱座特意带到位于筑地[1]的萨姆纳夫人担任园长的幼儿园。然而，星期六至星期日，必定到我母亲的娘家——坐落在本所的芥川家过夜。像这样出门的时候，“小初”穿的是就连在明治二十年代[2]都够时兴的西装。我记得上小学的时候，得到了给“小初”做西装的下脚布料。我把它们裹在人造橡胶玩具娃娃身上。那些下脚布料无一例外，全都是进口的平纹细白棉布，上面点缀着细碎的印花或乐器花样。

一个早春的星期日下午，“小初”一边在院子里踱来踱去，一边跟坐在房间里的伯妈说话。（我当然想象着当时姐姐依然穿着西装）

“伯妈，这棵树叫什么呀？”

“哪一棵树？”

---

1. 东京都中央区的一个街区。

2. 明治二十年至二十九年是 1887 年至 1896 年。

“这棵有花骨朵的树。”

我外婆家的院子里有一棵低矮的木瓜树。树枝耷拉到一口古老的井里。估计梳着小辫儿的“小初”杏眼圆睁，当时正凝视着枝子带刺儿的木瓜树吧。

“这棵树的名字跟你的一样。”

偏巧“小初”未能理解伯妈的戏谑语。

“那么，这棵树就叫作‘傻瓜树’喽。”

至今，只要有人提到“小初”，伯妈就反复地说她们之间曾经怎样一问一答。实际上，此外，“小初”说过的话，一句也没留存。大概这之后没过几天她就进了棺材。我不记得刻在小小的灵牌上的“小初”的戒名。然而，“小初”的忌辰是四月五日。玄妙的是，我对此记忆犹新。

不知为什么，我对这位姐姐——素昧平生的姐姐，有一种亲密感情。倘若“小初”至今健在，已经四十多岁了吧。过了不惑之年的“小初”那张脸也许活脱儿像是在坐落于芝的娘家二楼茫然地抽烟的母亲的脸吧。我时常宛若幻想一般觉得：弄不清是我母亲还是姐姐的一位四十来岁的女人，不知从何处守望着我的一生。难道这是喝咖啡啦、抽烟啦搞得疲惫不堪的我，神经遭到摧残了吗？抑或是超自然的力量借着什么机会出现在真实

的世界，并干出了这样的勾当吧？

三

由于母亲疯了，我刚生下来就到收养我的家来啦(那是舅父的家)，所以对亲生父亲也冷淡。我父亲经营牛奶铺，似乎是一位有些成功的人。教给我认识在当时而言还蛮时髦的水果与饮料的也统统是父亲。香蕉、冰激凌、菠萝、朗姆酒——或许还有其他的。我记得曾在当时坐落于新宿的牧场外边那棵槲树的树叶阴影下喝朗姆酒的往事。朗姆酒是酒精极少、橙黄色的饮料。

我父亲劝幼小的我吃喝如此新奇的东西，试图把我从收养我的家庭弄回来。我还记得有一天晚上，在大森[1]的鱼荣餐馆，父亲一边劝我吃冰激凌，一边露骨地说服我逃回到自个儿家来。说这番话的时候，我父亲发挥了巧言令色的本事。然而，遗憾的是他的劝说诱导一次也未奏效。因为我爱收养我的那一家的父母——尤其是舅妈。

我父亲还性急，屡次跟随便什么人吵架。我在中学

1. 是东京都大田区的一个街区。

三年级时，与父亲玩相扑，我用现代柔道的特殊招数巧妙地把他摔倒了。我父亲刚站起来就说“再来个回合”，并朝着我走过来。我再度没费什么力气就把他摔倒了。我父亲第三次一边说“再来个回合”，一边勃然变色猛扑过来。我的后母在观看——她是我母亲的妹妹，又是我父亲的继室——朝我使了两三个眼神。我与父亲较量了一番，故意摔了个四仰八叉。然而，倘若那时我没败给父亲，他必定要揪住我吧。

我二十八岁时——那时还在当教师，接到了“父住进医院”的电报，遂仓皇地从镰仓[1]直奔东京。我父亲是由于患流行性感冒而住进东京医院的。我与收养我的舅妈和后母在病房的角落住宿了约莫三天。这当儿我逐渐感到郁闷了。正在此时，跟我有交情的一位爱尔兰新闻记者打电话来邀请我到筑地的一家酒馆去吃饭。我以那位新闻记者最近要赴美国为借口，丢下奄奄一息的父亲，前往筑地的那家酒馆。

我们跟四五位艺伎一道，愉快地吃了日本风味的饭。大概是十点左右吃完的。有人从背后招呼我：“先

1. 神奈川县南部城市。

生。”我在中段止步，回头朝宽踏板的楼梯上边望着。一位恰好在场的艺伎聚精会神地俯视着我。我一言不发地走下楼梯。坐上停在正门外边的出租汽车。出租汽车立即开动了。然而，出现在我的脑海中的与其说是父亲，毋宁说是绾着娇艳的西式发髻的她的脸——尤其是她的眼睛。

我回到医院，只见父亲正等得不耐烦。不但如此，他让其他人全都离开，到两扇的屏风外边去。要么握住我的手，要么就抚摸它；谈起我不知道的往事——当年跟我母亲结婚时的事。左不过是与我母亲出门去买衣柜啦，购买了寿司啦，一些琐碎的事罢了。不过，正说着的时候，我的眼睑不知不觉地灼热起来了。眼泪也沿着我父亲那消瘦的脸蛋流下来。

我父亲在次日早晨没怎么痛苦地驾鹤西去，死前好像发疯了，说什么：“来了一艘军舰，瞧那些飘扬着的旗子！大伙儿都喊万岁吧！”我压根儿不记得自己父亲的丧礼情况。不过，依然记得把父亲的遗体护送到他本人之家时，春季的一轮大月亮的光照耀在灵柩车上。

四

今年三月中旬我还揣着怀炉时，隔了好久才第一次跟妻子一道去上坟。已经过去了这么久——然而，小小的坟墓自不待言，就连将枝子伸到坟墓上的一株赤松也没有变化。

添加在《点鬼簿》里的三个人的骸骨都埋在谷中墓地的角落里——而且在同一座墓碑下面。我想起了母亲的棺材被静悄悄地降下到这座墓碑下边时的往事。“小初”大概也是这样的。唯独我父亲——我记得父亲的骸骨发白、细碎，夹杂着金牙……

我并不喜欢上坟。倘若能忘掉，巴望把双亲与姐姐也忘记。然而，尤其是那一天，或许是身体衰弱的缘故，一边眺望早春的阳光中那座发黑的墓碑，一边思索：究竟他们三个人当中，谁幸福呢？

升腾起阳气
我独自住在
坟地外边

说实在的，我从来没有像这时那样，感到这么写的丈草[1]的心境逼近自己过。

（文洁若译于二〇一八年二月十四日）

1. 内腾丈草（1662—1704），江户前期的俳句诗人，“和歌”诗人。

傻子的一生

久米正雄君[1]：

此稿可否发表，什么时候在哪儿发表，我愿意完全委托给你。

稿中所出现的人物你大概都知道。但是发表之际，希望你不要加上注解。

我目前生活在最不幸的幸福当中。但奇怪的是我并不懊悔。我只是对有了我这样的恶夫、恶子、恶父的亲人感到遗憾。那么，再见了。在此稿中，我至少还不曾有意识地替自己辩护。

1. 久米正雄（1891—1952），日本小说家、剧作家。

最后再说一句：我之所以特地将此稿委托给你，乃是因为我相信你恐怕比任何人都更了解我。（一旦揭掉我这张城里人的皮）我在此稿中表现出的傻劲儿供你一笑。

昭和二年六月二十日

芥川龙之介

一　时代

那是某书店的二楼。年方二十的他登上靠在书架上的西式梯子，寻找新书。莫泊桑、波德莱尔[1]、斯特林堡、易卜生、萧伯纳、托尔斯泰……

天色逐渐黑下来了。他却还热心地继续读书脊上的字。那里陈列的，与其说是书籍，毋宁说是这个时代[2]本身。尼采、魏尔伦、龚古尔兄弟[3]、陀思妥耶夫斯基、

1. 波德莱尔（1821—1867），法国诗人。诗中歌咏死亡，充满悲观厌世情绪。
2. 文中所指为 19 世纪末，颓废派的时期。
3. 指埃德蒙·德·龚古尔（1822—1896）和茹尔·德·龚古尔（1830—1870），法国小说家，文学史上称“龚古尔兄弟”。

霍普特曼[1]、福楼拜……

他在薄暮中挣扎，数着他们的名字，可是书籍自然而然地淹没在阴郁的暮色中。他终于失去耐性，想从西式梯子上下来。他头上刚好悬着个秃灯泡，忽然亮了。他就立在梯子上，俯视在书籍之间移动的店员和顾客。他们显得怪渺小的，而且非常寒碜。

人生还不如波德莱尔的一行诗。

他立在梯子上，朝着这些人望了片刻。

二 母亲

疯子们都清一色地穿着灰衣服。宽阔的屋子因而越发显得忧郁。其中的一个对着风琴，热衷于弹赞美歌。同时，另外一个站在屋子正中间，与其说是跳舞，不如说是乱蹦着。

他和红光满面的医生一起看着这样的情景。十年前，他母亲也跟他们毫无二致。毫无——说实在的，他从他们的气味中嗅到了母亲的气味。

---

1. 霍普特曼（1862—1946），德国剧作家。

“那么，走吧？”

医生走在他的前面，沿着走廊进入一个房间。房间的角落里有个装满酒精的大玻璃瓶，里面浸着几副脑髓。他在其中的一副上发现了略微发白的东西，有些像是撒上了点蛋白。他同医生站着谈话，又想起了自己的母亲。

“这是 ×× 电灯公司的一个技师生前的脑髓。他一直认定自己是黑油油的大发电机。”

为了避开医生的视线，他就朝玻璃窗外面望去。除了插着空瓶碎片的砖墙以外，那里什么也没有。不过砖墙上长的薄薄青苔斑驳地泛着白色。

三 家

他住在郊外的一个二楼的房间里。由于地基松软了，这座房子的二楼有些倾斜。

他的姑妈常常跟他在楼上吵架。他的养父养母有时出面调解。可是他最爱这位姑妈。姑妈终身未嫁，当他二十岁的时候，她已接近六十岁了。

他在某郊外的楼上屡屡思索：莫非相爱的人就得彼此折磨吗？这当儿，他感到二楼歪斜得有点可怖。

四　东京

隅田川阴沉沉的。他从行驶中的小汽船窗口眺望向岛的樱树。在他眼里，盛开的樱花恍若一片败絮般令人忧郁。可是他在那些樱树中——江户时代以来的向岛的樱树中发现了他自己。

五　自我

他和他的前辈一起坐在某咖啡馆的桌边，不断地吸着纸烟。他不大开口讲话，却热心地听着前辈的话。

“今天乘了半天汽车。”

“有什么事情吗？”

他的前辈手托着腮，漫不经心地回答说：“没有什么事，只不过想坐坐罢了。”

这句话把他自己解放到不可知的世界——接近诸神的“自我”的世界。他觉得有点痛苦，同时也感到欢乐。

那个咖啡馆很小。牧羊神的相框下面却有一棵栽在赭色盆中的橡树，肥厚的叶片耷拉着。

六　病

潮风不断刮来，他摊开《英语大辞典》，手指划着找词条。

Talaria：生了翼的鞋，或作 Sandal。

Tale：故事。

Talipot：印度东部产的椰子。树干高达五十英尺至一百英尺，叶子可用于制伞、扇子、帽子等。七十年开花一次……

他凭想象清晰地描绘出这种椰子的花。他的喉咙从来没这么痒过，不由得往辞典上吐了口痰。痰？——那却不是痰。他想到短暂的生命，又一次想象着椰子花——在遥远的大海彼岸高高耸立的椰子花。

七　画

他突然地——实在是突然地……站在某书店的店头翻阅梵·高的画集时，他突然地领悟了画这个东西。当然，梵·高的画集无疑是影印版。他从影印版中也感到

了鲜明地浮现的大自然。

对这幅画的热情使他的眼界一新。他不知不觉间密切注意着树枝的弯曲和女人面颊的丰腴。

在一个下雨的秋日傍晚，他走过郊外的陆桥下面。陆桥对面的堤坝下停着一辆货运马车。他经过那里时，感到有人曾走过这条路。是谁呢？——无须问他本人。二十三岁的他，心目中浮现出一个割去了耳朵的荷兰人，叼着长烟斗，锐利的目光注视着这幅忧郁的风景画……

八　火花

他淋着雨，在柏油路上行走。雨下得相当大。在飞溅的雨水中，他嗅到了橡胶雨衣的气味。

眼前的一根架空线冒出紫色火花。他格外感动。他的上衣口袋里藏着准备在同人杂志上发表的原稿。他冒雨走着，再次仰望了一下后面的架空线。

架空线依然放出耀眼的火花。他展望人生，并没有特别稀罕的东西。但是只有这紫色的火花——只有这可怕的空中的火花，哪怕用生命来换取，他也想把它抓住。

九　尸体

那些尸体的拇指上都挂着穿上铁丝的牌子，上面记着姓名、年龄等等。他的朋友弯着腰，灵活地运用解剖刀，开始剥一具尸体脸上的皮。皮下布满了美丽的黄色脂肪。

他望着那具尸体。为了完成一个短篇——以王朝时代为背景的一个短篇，他非这么做不可。可是，像腐烂了的杏子一样的尸臭是难闻的。他的朋友皱起眉头，静静地动着解剖刀。

“近来尸体也不够用。”他的朋友说。

不知什么时候，他早已准备好了答复：“如果尸体不够用，我就会没有任何恶意地去杀人。”可是他当然只把这话放在心里。

十　先生

他在一棵大槲树下读着先生的书。槲树沐浴在秋天的阳光下，连一片叶子也不动。远处的空中有一架吊着

玻璃秤盘的天平，刚好保持平衡——他边读着先生的书，边遐想着这样的情景……

十一　拂晓

天逐渐亮了。有一次，他在某街的拐角望着广阔的市场。市场上熙熙攘攘的人和车子都染成了玫瑰色。

他点燃一支纸烟，安详地走进市场。一条黑色瘦狗突然向他吠起来。可是他不惊慌。他甚至爱起那条狗来。

市场正中有一棵法国梧桐树，树枝向四面挓挲着。他站在树干下，透过树枝仰望高空。正好在他头顶上空，闪烁着一颗星星。

这是他二十五岁的时候——会见先生以后的第三个月。

十二　军港

潜水艇内部是阴暗的。周围都是机器，他弯着腰，透过小小的方镜望去。映在方镜里的是明亮的军港风光。

“那边还可以看到‘金刚’呢。”一个海军高级军官

对他说。

他看着方镜上的小军舰，不知怎的，忽然想起了荷兰芹菜——每份三毛钱的牛排上也有荷兰芹菜，散发着清香。

十三　先生之死

雨后起了风，他在一个新车站的站台上走着。天刚蒙蒙亮。站台那面，三四名铁路工人一齐抡着镐，高声唱着什么。

雨后的风吹散了工人的歌声和他的感情。他拿着没有点燃的香烟，感到近于欢乐的痛苦。“先生病危”的电报揣在大衣兜里……

这时，从对面松山的背阴处，早上六点的上行列车拖着一缕轻烟，蜿蜒向这边驶来。

十四　结婚

婚后第二天他就数落妻子道：“刚来就浪费可不行啊。”然而，这种数落的话，与其说是他自己要说的，不

如说是他的姑妈叫他“说”的。当然，他的妻子不但向他本人，也向他的姑妈赔了不是。为他买来的那钵黄水仙花就摆在她前面……

十五　他们

在大芭蕉叶的宽阔阴影下，他们和平地生活着——他们的家在从东京乘火车要足足一小时的海滨某镇上。

十六　枕头

他枕着散发玫瑰叶香的怀疑主义，读着阿纳托尔·法朗士的书。可是，他没有注意到枕中还有半人半马神。

十七　蝴蝶

在充满海藻气味的风中，一只蝴蝶在蹁跹飞舞。一眨眼的工夫，他感到这只蝴蝶的翅膀碰了一下他那干燥的嘴唇。可是沾在他嘴唇上的翅粉却在几年后还闪着光。

十八　月

他在某饭店的台阶上偶然遇见了她。就连在这样的白昼，她的脸也跟在月光下一样。他目送着她（他俩素昧平生），感到从来没有过的寂寞……

十九　人工翼

他从阿纳托尔·法朗士转向十八世纪的哲学家去了，但是他没有接近卢梭。那或许是他本人的一面——容易感情用事的一面跟卢梭相近之故。他却去接近跟他本身的另一面——富于冷静的理智的一面——相近的《天真汉》[1]的哲学家了。

对二十九岁的他来说，人生已经一点也不光明了。可是伏尔泰给了这样的他以人工翼。

他张开这人工翼，轻而易举地飞上天空。同时，理智之光照耀的人生的悲欢沉沦在他的眼底下。他向穷街陋巷投以讽刺与微笑，穿过一无遮拦的太空，径直飞向

1.《天真汉》是法国启蒙思想家、哲学家、作家伏尔泰（1694—1778）的哲理小说。

太阳。他似乎忘记了古代希腊人因这样的人工翼被阳光晒化而终于落进海里死去的事[1]……

二十　桎梏

由于他要到某报社去工作，他们夫妇就跟他的养父养母同住在一座房子里了。他依靠的是写在黄纸上的合同。后来才知道，报社对这份合同不承担任何义务，只由他承担义务。

二十一　狂人的女儿

两辆人力车在冷冷清清的阴天的乡间道路上跑着。海风习习，这条路显然通向海边。他坐在后面这辆人力车上，边纳闷着为什么自己对这次的幽会兴致索然，边思索是什么把他引到这里来的。这绝不是恋爱。倘若不是恋爱——他为了回避这个答复，不得不想：总之，我

1. 见希腊神话中的故事《代达罗斯和伊卡洛斯》。伊卡洛斯和他的父亲代达罗斯一起逃离克瑞忒，伊卡洛斯不听父亲的话，飞近太阳，人工翼上的蜡被晒化，坠海而死。

们是平等的。

坐在前面那辆人力车上的是一个狂人的女儿。不仅如此，她的妹妹是因嫉妒而自杀的。

——事到如今，怎么也没办法了。

他对这个狂人的女儿——她只有强烈的动物本能——已经感到某种憎恶了。

这当儿，两辆人力车经过有咸腥气味的墓地外面。粘着蚝壳的矮树篱里面，有几座黑黝黝的石塔。他眺望着在那些石塔后面微微闪烁的海洋，不知怎的，忽然对她的丈夫——没能抓住她的心的丈夫，感到蔑视……

二十二　某画家

那是某杂志的插图。一只公鸡的水墨画表现出明显的个性。他向某友人打听这位画家的情况。

大约一周后，这位画家访问了他。在他的一生中，这是一件颇不寻常的事情。他在这位画家身上发现了谁都不知道的那一面。不但如此，还发现了连画家本人也一直不知道的画家的灵魂。

在一个微寒的秋日傍晚，他因看到一株玉米，蓦地

联想起这位画家。长得高高的玉米，披着粗糙的叶子，培在根部的土里露出像神经那样纤细的根须。这无疑又是容易受伤的他的自画像。可是这样的发现只有使他忧郁罢了。

——已经晚了。可是到了节骨眼儿上……

二十三　她

某广场前面，暮色苍茫。他的身体发着低烧，在广场上踱步。晴空略呈银色，大厦林立，窗口灯火辉煌。

他在路边停下脚步，等候她到来。大约过了五分钟，她好像有些憔悴似的向他走来。她看到了他的脸，就微笑着说：“累啦。”他们并肩在依稀有些亮光的广场上走着。对他们来说，这是第一次。为了跟她在一起，他无论抛掉什么都在所不惜。

他们乘上汽车后，她凝视着他的脸说：“你不后悔吗？”他斩钉截铁地说：“不后悔。”她按着他的手说道：“我也不后悔。”这样讲的时候，她的脸好像沐浴在月光下。

二十四　分娩

他伫立在纸隔扇旁边，俯视着穿白色手术衣的一名接生婆在给婴儿洗澡。每当肥皂浸进眼里，婴儿就可爱地反复皱起眉头，还不断地大声哭。他一面觉得婴儿的气味有点像鼠崽子，一面不由得深刻地想道：“为什么这娃娃也出生了呢？生到这个充满俗世之苦的世界上来——为什么他命中注定要有我这个爸爸呢？”

而且这是他的妻子头胎生的男孩。

二十五　斯特林堡

他站在房间门口，看着开着石榴花的月光底下几个衣冠不整的中国人在打麻将。然后回到房间里，在矮矮的油灯下开始读《痴人的告白》。可是还没有读上两页，就不知不觉苦笑起来——斯特林堡在给情妇伯爵夫人的信中，写着和他差不离的谎言……

二十六　古代

彩色剥落了的佛像、天人、马和莲花座几乎使他为之倾倒。他仰望着它们，把一切抛在脑后。甚至忘记了他本人侥幸得以摆脱狂人的女儿……

二十七　斯巴达式训练

他同他的朋友在一条巷子里走着。一辆上篷的人力车径直迎面跑来。而且出人意料的是车上坐的正是昨晚的她。在这样的白昼，她的面容恍若沐浴在月光下。当着他朋友的面，他们当然连招呼也没打。

“真漂亮。”他的朋友这样说。

他望着巷子尽头的春天的山，毫不犹豫地回答说：“是啊，真漂亮。”

二十八　杀人

乡间道路沐浴在阳光下，散发着牛粪的臭气。他揩着汗，踏着上坡路走去。道路两旁飘着熟麦的香气。

“杀吧，杀吧……”他不知不觉间嘴里反复嘟囔着。杀谁呢？——这他是清楚的。他想起一个极卑鄙的留平头的男子。

黄色麦地的那面，不知何时露出了一座天主教堂的圆屋顶……

二十九　形象

那是一把铁制酒壶。这把细纹酒壶使他懂得了“造型”的美。

三十　雨

他在大床上同她聊着天。寝室窗外下着雨。在这场雨中，木棉花说不上什么时候就会烂掉吧。她的面容仍像是沐浴在月光下。可是同她交谈，他不免感到无聊。他匍匐着，静静地点起一支纸烟，想起同她一起生活已有七年了。

“我爱着这个女人吗？”他问他自己道。

“我还爱着。”——这个答复使注视着自己的他也感

到意外。

三十一　大地震

那种气味和熟透了的杏子差不多。他在火灾后的废墟上走着，微微嗅到这样的气味，于是想道：炎天的腐尸，气味居然也不太难闻。可是当他站在尸骸累累的池畔望去的时候，才发现“鼻子发酸”这句话在感觉上绝不是夸张的。尤其使他动情的是十二三岁的小孩的尸体。他看着那具尸体，有点觉得羡慕。他想起“上帝所爱者不长命”这句话。他的姐姐和异母兄弟的家都焚毁了，而且他的姐夫是犯了伪证罪而缓期服刑的……

他站在灰烬中，不由得深深地想道：人人都死掉才好呢。

三十二　打架

他同异母兄弟扭打起来了。他弟弟无疑由于他的缘故经常受到压迫。同时，他也因为弟弟而失掉了自由。他的亲戚一个劲儿地对他的弟弟说：“你要学他。”然而

这不啻是把他本人的手脚都绑了起来。他们扭作一团，终于滚到廊子上了。他还记得，廊外的庭院中有一棵百日红，在酝酿着一场雨的天空下开着红彤彤的花。

三十三　英雄

不知什么时候，他从伏尔泰家的窗口仰望着高山。那挂着冰河的山上，连秃鹰的影子也看不见。可是有一个身材矮小的俄罗斯人在顽强地沿着山路攀登。

夜幕降临到伏尔泰家后，他在明亮的灯光下回忆着攀登山路的俄罗斯人的身姿，写了这样一首有教化目的的诗：

你比谁都恪守十诫，
又比谁都违反十诫。

你比谁都爱护民众，
又比谁都轻视民众。

你比谁都富于理想，

又比谁都了解现实。

你是我们东洋诞生的，
散发草花香气的电气机车。

三十四　色彩

三十岁的他不知什么时候爱上了某块空地。那里，长着青苔的地面上只散着一些残砖碎瓦。可是在他眼里这与塞尚[1]的风景画没有什么两样。

他忽然想起了七八年前他的激情。同时发现他在七八年前是不懂得色彩的。

三十五　假人

他打算过一种激烈到不论何时死去也不会后悔的生活。可是在养父养母和姑妈面前，他的日子依然过得很拘谨。这就使他的生活形成了阴阳两面。他看见

1. 塞尚（1839—1906），法国画家，后期印象派的代表人物。

立在某西服店里的一个人体模型，就想到究竟他自己在多大程度上像这个模型。但是意识之外的他——可以说是第二个他，早已把这样的心情写入一篇短篇小说里了。

三十六　倦怠

他同一个大学生在长满狗尾草的野地上行走。

“你们仍有旺盛的生活欲吧？”

“嗯……可是你也……”

“可是我没有了。只是有创作欲罢了。”

这是他的真情。说实在的，他不知不觉间已对生活失去了兴趣。

“创作欲也是生活欲吧。”

他没有回答。曾几何时，野地的红穗上清晰地映现出一座喷火山。他觉得有些羡慕这座喷火山。可是他自己也莫名其所以然……

三十七　过来人

他遇到了在才力上也能够同他匹敌的女人。可是他写了《过来人》等抒情诗，才摆脱了这个危机。这是一种百无聊赖的心情，宛如把冻在树干上的闪闪发光的雪拍了下来。

草笠随风舞，
飘摇落道旁；
我名何所惜，
但愿君名扬。

三十八　复仇

那是某饭店的阳台，周围满是刚萌芽的树木。他在那里画着画，哄一个少年玩。这是七年前分手的狂人的女儿的独生子。

狂人的女儿点燃纸烟，看着他们玩。他在心情沉重地继续描绘火车和飞机。幸亏这个少年不是他的儿子。可是，使他感到痛苦的莫过于这个少年叫他“叔叔”。

少年不知跑到哪儿去了，狂人的女儿边抽着烟，边带点媚态地对他说：“那孩子不像你吗？”

“不像。第一……”

“可是，还有胎教的说法呢。”

他默不作声，眼睛望着一旁。可是他心里并非没有残忍的愿望，恨不得把他掐死……

三十九　镜子

他在某咖啡馆的一个角落里同朋友谈话。他的朋友吃着烤苹果，谈论着近来天气寒冷之类的话。他突然感到这样的话里有矛盾。

“你还是独身呀。”

“不，下个月就结婚。”

他不由得默不作声了。嵌在咖啡馆墙壁上的镜子映出他无数的形象。冷冰冰的，像威胁什么似的……

四十　问答

你为什么要攻击现代的社会制度？

因为我看到了资本主义所产生的罪恶。

罪恶？我还只当你分辨不出善恶的差别呢。那么，你的生活呢？

——他就这样同天使一问一答。当然是体体面面地戴着大礼帽的天使……

四十一　病

他患了失眠病，并且体力也开始衰弱了。好几位医生各自给他的病做了两三种诊断：胃酸过多、胃弛缓、干性肋膜炎、神经衰弱、慢性结膜炎、脑疲劳……

可是他知道自己的病源。那就是对他自己感到羞愧，同时又害怕他们的心情。害怕他们——害怕他所蔑视的社会！

在一个要下雪的阴沉的下午，他在某咖啡馆的一个角落里衔着点燃了的雪茄烟，倾听对面留声机放出的音乐。乐声沁人心脾。等到那段音乐结束后，他就走到留声机前，看看唱片上贴的说明：《魔笛》——莫扎特。[1]

1. 原文为英文。

他顿时领悟了。破了十诫的莫扎特也还是有过苦闷的。可是，该不至于像他这样……他垂着头，静静地回到自己的桌边。

四十二　众神的笑声

在春光明媚的松林中，三十五岁的他边踱步边回忆着自己两三年前写过的话：

我最同情的是神不能自杀。

四十三　夜

夜幕又快降临了。要闹天气了，半明半暗中，海上浪花滚滚。在这样的天空下，他同妻子第二次结婚了。这给他们带来了欢乐，同时又带来痛苦。三个孩子和他们一起看着海上的闪电。他的妻子抱着一个孩子，好像忍着眼泪。

“那边有一只船。”

“嗯。”

“樯杆断了的船。”

四十四　死

他趁着独自睡觉的机会，把腰带挂在窗棂子上想自缢。可是把脖子伸进带子时忽然又怕死了。并不是害怕死的那一瞬间的痛苦。他第二次自缢时拿着怀表测试缢死的时间。稍感痛苦以后，神志就有些恍惚了。只要过了这一关，准会进入死境。他看了看表针，发现感到痛苦的过程为一分二十几秒。窗棂子外一片漆黑。从黑暗中传来了粗犷的鸡鸣。

四十五　Divan[1]

Divan 即将再次给他的心灵倾注以新的力量。那是他所不知道的“东洋的歌德”。他看见超脱一切善恶，悠然站在彼岸的歌德，感到近乎绝望的羡慕。在他眼里，诗人歌德比诗人基督更伟大。在这位诗人的心中，除了

1. 英语：诗集（尤指用波斯文或阿拉伯文写的个人诗集）。

阿克罗波利斯[1]和各各他[2]之外，还有阿拉伯玫瑰花在怒放。倘若多少有力量追踪这位诗人的足迹的话……他读完诗集，当极为激动的情绪平息以后，不禁深深蔑视自己，因为他在生活中就像宦官一样。

四十六　谎言

他姐夫的自杀猝然使他受了打击。今后连姐姐一家人也得由他来照顾了。至少对他来说，未来就像日暮那样昏暗。他对自己精神上的破产有一种近乎冷笑的感觉（他完全明白自己的罪孽和弱点），继续阅读各种书籍。可是连卢梭的《忏悔录》也充满英雄的谎言。尤其是《新生》[3]——他从来没有遇见过像《新生》的主人公那样老奸巨猾的伪善者。可是只有弗朗索瓦·维庸[4]浸透了他的心。他在几篇诗里发现了“美丽的男性”。

---

1. 阿克罗波利斯是雅典的卫城。
2. 各各他是耶稣被钉上十字架的地方。
3.《新生》（1918—1919）是岛崎藤村的自传体长篇小说，描写作者做出了背离社会道德的事情后，交代了事实经过，从而获得“新生”。
4. 弗朗索瓦·维庸（1431—约 1463），法国抒情诗人，贫民出身，一生颠沛流离。

等待绞刑的维庸的形象出现在他的梦里。他几次差点儿像维庸那样坠入人生的底层。但是他的境遇和体力不允许这样。他渐渐衰弱下去，恰似从前斯威夫特[1]见到过的从树梢枯萎起来的树木那样……

四十七　玩火

她容光焕发，犹如晨光照耀下的薄冰似的。他对她抱有好感，但是没有恋爱的感觉，而且连碰也没碰过她的身体。

“听说你想死。”

“是——不，与其说想死，不如说活腻了。”

他们这样一问一答，约好一起死。

“这是精神自杀。”

“双双精神自杀。”

他对他自己这样镇静自若，不由得感到奇怪。

1. 斯威夫特（1667—1745），英国讽刺作家，生于爱尔兰贫苦家庭，著有《格列佛游记》。他曾参加爱尔兰人民反抗英国统治者的斗争，晚年发疯。

四十八　死

他没有同她一起死。至今连碰也没碰过她的身体这一点，似乎使他感到满意。她若无其事地时常同他谈，并且把她带着的一瓶氰化钾递给他，还说：“有了这个，彼此心里都有仗势了。”

那确实使他心里有了仗势。他独自坐在藤椅上，看着柯树的嫩叶，不由得反复思索死亡将给予他的和平。

四十九　剥制的天鹅

他想尽最后的力量写自传。可是这对他来说竟然并不容易。那是由于他还残留着自尊心、怀疑主义和利害打算。他不得不轻蔑这样的自己。可是另一方面，他又不由自主地想：如果剥开一层皮来看，谁都是一样的。他总是想，《诗与真实》这个书名好像是一切自传的书名。他还清楚地知道，文艺作品不一定使人人都感动。他还产生了这样的念头：只有那些与他的生涯相近并且和他相似的人们才会为他的作品所感动。因此，他决定简短地把自己的《诗与真实》写出来。

他写完《傻子的一生》后，偶然在某旧家具店看见了剥制的天鹅。它伸长了颈立着，连发黄的羽毛也被蛀蚀了。他回想自己的一生，不禁热泪盈眶，发出冷笑。他的前途不是发疯就是自杀。他独自在日落的街上走着，决心等待慢慢把他毁灭的命运的到来。

五十　俘虏

他的朋友之一发疯了。他对这个朋友一向有某种亲近的感觉。因为他比别人更深刻地理解这个朋友的孤独——快活的假面掩盖下的孤独。这个朋友发疯后他去看望过两三次。

“你和我都给恶魔附体了——给所谓世纪末的恶魔附体了。”

这位朋友曾低声对他这样说。听说两三天以后，这位朋友在去某温泉旅馆的途中，甚至吃起玫瑰花来了。这个朋友住院后，他想起了过去曾送给这个朋友一座赤陶半身像。那是这个朋友所喜欢的《钦差大臣》一书的作者的半身像。他想起果戈理也是发疯而死的，不由得感到冥冥之中有一股力量在支配他们。

他已筋疲力竭之际，偶尔读到拉迪盖[1]临终的话，又一次觉得听见了众神的笑声。那句话说："神兵来捉我。"他想与他的迷信和感伤主义做斗争。可是从肉体上来说，他已经不可能进行任何斗争了。"世纪末的恶魔"无疑正在摧残他。他对虔信神的中世纪的人们感到羡慕。可是他终究不可能信神——信仰神的爱。连科克托[2]都是信神的啊！

五十一　败北

他执笔的手颤抖起来了，甚至还流了口水。除非服用零点八毫克的佛罗那[3]，他的头脑没有一次清醒过，而且清醒也不过半小时或一小时。他只有在幽暗中挨着时光，直好像是将一把崩了刃的细剑当拐杖拄着。

一九二七年六月，遗稿

（文学朴　译）

---

1. 拉迪盖（1903—1923），法国小说家、诗人。
2. 科克托（1889—1963），法国诗人、小说家。
3. 佛罗那是一种安眠药。

企鹅经典：小黑书　第一辑

01. 贝尔科洛蕾夫人与神父

[意] 薄伽丘

02. 泄密的心

[美] 爱伦·坡

03. 醋栗

[俄] 契诃夫

04. 一个人需要许多土地吗?

[俄] 列夫·托尔斯泰

05. 一颗简单的心

[法] 福楼拜

06. 傻子的一生

[日] 芥川龙之介

07. 萎缩的胳膊

[英] 托马斯·哈代

08. 樱花树下的清酒

[日] 吉田兼好

09. 虎! 虎!

[英] 威廉·布莱克

10. 给一个青年诗人的十封信

[奥] 里尔克

Penguin Little Black Classics Vol. I

01. GIOVANNI BOCCACCIO
Mrs Rosie and the Priest

02. EDGAR ALLAN POE
The Tell-Tale Heart

03. ANTON CHEKHOV
Gooseberries

04. LEO TOLSTOY
How Much Land Does a Man Need?

05. GUSTAVE FLAUBERT
A Simple Heart

06. RYUNOSUKE AKUTAGAWA
The Life of a Stupid Man

07. THOMAS HARDY
The Withered Arm

08. KENKO
A Cup of Sake Beneath the Cherry Trees

09. WILLIAM BLAKE
Tyger Tyger

10. RAINER MARIA RILKE
Letters to a Young Poet